A WATERY DEATH

The boiling, churning waters tossed the keelboat around like a cork in a child's bath. With a sharp snap, Touch the Sky's pole became wedged between two boulders and broke. At the same moment, one of the Creoles manning the cordelles slipped on the sharp bank and tumbled down into the water, injuring his left leg.

Seeing that the Nose Talker was in no immediate danger of drowning, Touch the Sky leaped into the river, fought his way to the bank, and gripped the thick cordelle in the voyageur's place.

"Heave!" Jackson shouted, fear replacing the surliness in his voice.

For a moment the *Sioux Princess* balanced between sure destruction and uncertain salvation. Then it bounced into the narrower, calmer channel.

The heavy keelboat missed crushing Touch the Sky to death by inches. But the hapless crew member trapped in the river was not so lucky. As the young brave watched horrified, the injured Creole was instantly crushed to a human paste against the rocks.

The *Cheyenne Series:*

BLOOD ON THE PLAINS

JUDD COLE

LEISURE BOOKS NEW YORK CITY

A LEISURE BOOK®

May 1993

Published by

Dorchester Publishing Co., Inc.
276 Fifth Avenue
New York, NY 10001

Printed in the United States of America.

Prologue

Twenty winters before the Bluecoats fought against the Graycoats in the great war between white men, Running Antelope and his Northern Cheyenne band were massacred by pony soldiers at the Platte River. The lone survivor was Running Antelope's infant son. His Shaiyena name was lost forever. He grew up as Matthew Hanchon in the Wyoming Territory settlement of Bighorn Falls, adopted son of John and Sarah Hanchon.

The Hanchons loved him as their own and treated him well. But their love could not overcome the hatred many other settlers felt for Matthew. Tragedy struck in 1856, when Matthew turned 16 and fell in love with Kristen, daughter of wealthy rancher Hiram Steele. Matthew was viciously beaten by one of Steele's wranglers. Then Seth Carlson, a young cavalry officer with plans to marry Kristen, threatened to ruin the Hanchons'

mercantile business unless Matthew cleared out
for good.

But when he fled north to the Powder River and
Cheyenne country, he was immediately captured
by Yellow Bear's tribe and sentenced to death as
a spy for the Long Knives.

But Arrow Keeper, the tribe's medicine man,
had experienced a recent vision and recognized
the birthmark buried past the youth's hairline:
a mulberry-colored arrowhead, the mark of the
warrior. According to Arrow Keeper's medicine
vision, this tall youth was marked by destiny to
lead his people in one great, final victory against
their white enemy.

Arrow Keeper buried Matthew's white name and
renamed the towering youth Touch the Sky. But
Black Elk instantly hated the stranger—especially after Honey Eater, daughter of Chief Yellow Bear, made love talk with him. Black Elk's
fiery-tempered cousin, Wolf Who Hunts Smiling,
walked between Touch the Sky and the campfire—
thus announcing his intention of killing the suspected spy.

Even after Touch the Sky and his white friend
Corey Robinson cleverly saved the Cheyenne village from annihilation by Pawnee, he was not
fully accepted by the tribe. Then whiskey traders
invaded Indian country, led by the ruthless Henri
Lagace.

Lagace kidnapped Honey Eater and threatened
to kill her if the Cheyenne went on the warpath
against him. A small war party, led by Black Elk,
was sent into the heavily fortified white strong-
hold.

Touch the Sky was warned, in a medicine vision,
that he must defy Black Elk's orders or Honey

Eater would die. He deserted the war party and infiltrated the white camp on his own. Honey Eater was freed and Touch the Sky killed Lagace. But much of his valor went unwitnessed, and many in the tribe remained unconvinced of his loyalty.

Their suspicions were heightened when he rushed back to the river-bend settlement of Bighorn Falls to help his white parents. Rancher Hiram Steele and Lt. Seth Carlson had first teamed up to drive the Hanchons out of the mercantile trade; now they had begun a bloody campaign to drive them from their new mustang spread.

Touch the Sky was torn in his loyalties. Chief Yellow Bear lay dying, and Honey Eater could not live alone if he crossed over to the Land of Ghosts—meaning she would have to accept Black Elk's bride-price and marry him if Yellow Bear died. But in the end Touch the Sky left, realizing his white parents' battle was his battle.

Assisted by his friend Little Horse, Touch the Sky defeated his parents' enemies. But seeing his parents and Kristen again left Touch the Sky feeling hopelessly trapped between two worlds, at home in neither. His tragic plight worsened when he returned to the Cheyenne camp. Not only had Yellow Bear died, forcing Honey Eater to marry Black Elk. But spies had watched Touch the Sky during his absence. They'd mistaken Touch the Sky's meetings with the sympathetic cavalry officer Tom Riley as proof the Cheyenne was a traitor to his people.

Arrow Keeper, acting chief since Yellow Bear's death, used his power to intervene and save the youth. Arrow Keeper still believed in the original vision which foretold Touch the Sky's greatness.

Now, he realized, the youth must seek the vision himself, and thus accept his destiny as a Cheyenne and resolve the agony of being the eternal outsider.

The old shaman sent Touch the Sky to sacred Medicine Lake for a vision quest. The journey became an epic struggle to survive Pawnee, starvation, flash floods, life-threatening wounds, a riled grizzly, and an assassination attempt ordered by Black Elk. But Touch the Sky finally experienced the key vision. Profoundly moved by the images and secrets of the Vision Way, he accepted once and for all his place as a Cheyenne.

When he came back to camp, Arrow Keeper announced that Touch the Sky had the gift of visions and would be trained in the shaman arts. Then Touch the Sky discovered to his joy that Honey Eater still loved only him despite her marriage to Black Elk. This strengthened his resolve. He still had many enemies, but he was home to stay. Anyone who wanted to drive him away now must either kill him or die in the attempt.

Chapter 1

"Now comes Catch the Hawk's band!" shouted the camp crier, racing up and down on his dappled gray pony between the lodges and tipis. "All hail our Shaiyena brothers!"

The tall youth named Touch the Sky joined the rest of those already gathered in a rousing cheer of welcome as the last of the ten far-flung Cheyenne bands rode into the temporary Tongue River Valley camp. Catch the Hawk's tribe, whose summer camp was on the Rosebud, broke into an answering chorus of whoops, shouts, and songs. The warriors had donned their single-horned crow-feather bonnets in honor of the chief-renewal ceremony.

"This is always the way it is when the Cheyenne people come together as one," explained Arrow Keeper proudly to Touch the Sky. The old medicine man's weather-lined face was divided by a wide smile. "The Cheyenne people live in widely scattered camps. Only during the chief-renewal or the Sun Dance ceremonies of the warm moons do they erect their lodges in one camp."

Touch the Sky watched, his keen black eyes wide with curiosity. He had a strong, hawk nose and wore his black hair in long, loose locks, except where it was cut short over his brow to keep his vision clear.

Already the newest arrivals were gathering by clans to set up their tipis. Besides the Cheyenne, the camp was swollen with visitors from other Plains tribes friendly to the Cheyenne: the Dakota, the Arapaho, the Cheyenne's Teton Sioux cousins.

"My blood is Cheyenne like yours, Father," said Touch the Sky, who had 18 winters behind him. "But so much is new to me. I fear I will make mistakes during the ceremonies."

Old Arrow Keeper nodded, pulling his red Hudson's Bay blanket tighter around his gaunt figure. The shaman had served as acting chief since the death of Chief Yellow Bear. Now the Council of Forty, known simply as the Headmen, had appointed Gray Thunder of the Wolverine Clan as their new chief. The chief-renewal was an occasion of grand feasting and dancing, of much gift-giving. The poor would profit handsomely, as it was an honored custom to give horses, robes, and other things of value to the needy.

"You will make some mistakes," Arrow Keeper said. "Mighty oaks do not spring up overnight. There is much to learn. It takes many winters to develop the proper spirit, to learn the skills of a tribe shaman.

"Think back to the time when you left your white parents and rode into our country alone. You made many mistakes as a warrior in training also. But today even your worst enemies within the tribe admit you are one of our best fighters."

These words heartened the youth. Arrow Keeper had recently announced that Touch the Sky was to be his shaman apprentice. With this decision, the elder had sent a clear message to Touch the Sky's many enemies within the tribe. Despite the claims of Black Elk, Wolf Who Hunts Smiling, and others, who still accused Touch the Sky of being a spy for the Bluecoats, Arrow Keeper believed in him. Though he had been raised by whites, Arrow Keeper was convinced he was straight-arrow Shaiyena.

Further conversation was difficult now as the cheering and shouting and singing swelled like a gathering avalanche. The cleared space in the middle of the huge makeshift camp was nearly a mile across. The lodges now numbered between five and six hundred, each facing east. The circle itself was a symbolic tipi with the open door to the rising sun.

Soon Touch the Sky would assist Arrow Keeper in conducting the huge Sun Dance, a celebration of the warm moons and the hunts to come as well as the annual tribute to the all-important horses. For this important occasion the tall youth had donned his best beaded leggings and clout. Several eagle-tail feathers adorned his war bonnet, one for each time he had counted coup against an enemy. He wore an elk-tooth necklace, and his face and body were painted with red-bank war paint. He would paint and dress again for the actual dance.

Arrow Keeper touched the youth's arm, then led him to his tipi. The shaman lifted the elkskin flap over the entrance. He stepped inside, then emerged again and handed something to Touch the Sky. The old man leaned close to his young friend's ear so he could be heard above the din.

"Here is a mountain-lion skin. I used to wear this in the parades. It is blessed with strong magic for anyone who has the gift of visions, as you have. Now I give it to you, little brother."

The tawny fur robe was soft and beautiful. When Touch the Sky tried to thank Arrow Keeper, the elder stopped him.

"We live on through the tribe. Boiled sassafras no longer comforts my old bones. Soon I must join Chief Yellow Bear in the Land of Ghosts. But the spirit of Arrow Keeper will live in Touch the Sky. Give this robe to your son, little brother, when your hair has turned to white frost like mine."

Upon mentioning Yellow Bear, Arrow Keeper had automatically made the cut-off sign as one did when speaking of the dead. Now, exhausted by the long days of celebration, the old shaman stepped back into his tipi to rest and prepare for the Sun Dance.

His mind full of many tangled thoughts, Touch the Sky headed toward his own tipi to put away his new gift. He was skirting the huge buffalo-rope pony corral when suddenly he drew up short. A trio of Cheyenne bucks had crossed his path. He recognized them as Black Elk, Swift Canoe, and Wolf Who Hunts Smiling.

"Our new 'shaman' has acquired some finery," said Black Elk, the oldest of the three.

He was a fierce young warrior with 22 winters behind him. One ear had been severed by a Blue-coat saber, then later sewn back on with buffalo sinew. This lent him an especially fierce aspect.

"Perhaps," added Black Elk, "he may use this skin as the bride-price for his own squaw instead of attempting to steal a bride from his betters."

Despite his impassive face, these mocking words were bitter. Black Elk had recently performed the squaw-taking ceremony with Honey Eater, daughter of the great peace chief Yellow Bear. Touch the Sky knew that the jealous Black Elk suspected him of holding Honey Eater in his blanket—making love talk to her despite her marriage.

Touch the Sky waited a few heartbeats until the first flush of anger had passed. He had recently made a sojourn to sacred Medicine Lake in the Black Hills. There, a powerful medicine vision had convinced him that his place was with the Cheyenne. Now he was determined to do everything he possibly could to convince his enemies he was a loyal Cheyenne, not a double-tongued spy for the hairy faces.

"Black Elk is my war leader and the brave who taught me the arts of combat," said Touch the Sky. "Thus, I freely admit he is my better. But never have I attempted to steal any brave's squaw."

These conciliatory words had little impact on Black Elk's scowl. But Touch the Sky was gratified to note that Black Elk's younger cousin, Wolf Who Hunts Smiling, seemed more subdued around him, less hateful and insulting than formerly.

They were still far from friends. But at least Wolf Who Hunts Smiling had revoked his long-standing threat to kill Touch the Sky. This was because Touch the Sky had bravely interceded during a Pawnee attack, saving the lives of Wolf Who Hunts Smiling and Swift Canoe. Now Wolf Who Hunts Smiling maintained a stone-eyed silence around him. But Touch the Sky knew the young warrior was intensely ambitious and he feared they must someday clash.

Swift Canoe, however, had not witnessed Touch

the Sky's bravery because he had lain in a creek bed wounded. And he still blamed Touch the Sky, wrongly, for causing the death of his twin brother, True Son. Unfortunately, Gray Thunder, the new peace chief, was a member of Swift Canoe's Wolverine Clan. Like Swift Canoe, Gray Thunder was suspicious of Touch the Sky.

Now Swift Canoe spoke up. "Arrow Keeper would teach this spy all the sacred secrets of our tribe. He will let him handle the sacred Medicine Arrows—yet he has contaminated himself forever by shedding tribe blood!"

"The only blood I have ever shed," said Touch the Sky, holding his face expressionless in the Indian way, "was spilled defending my life or protecting my tribe. I had nothing to do with the death of your brother."

"You speak in a wolf bark, white man's dog!"

Touch the Sky felt warm blood creeping into his face. Before he could reply, a familiar figure glided up close beside him.

"If it is three against one, brother," said his friend Little Horse, "I am here to help even the fight."

Little Horse was small, but quick and sure in his movements and built sturdy like a war pony. His steadfast loyalty to Touch the Sky had cost him friends in the tribe. But no one doubted his courage or ability in battle.

Copying the elders, Touch the Sky stepped back and folded his arms to show he was at peace. "There will be no fight, brother. This is a time of rejoicing. Come! Let us prepare for the Sun Dance."

Several naked Cheyenne children were playing near the river bend when the *Sioux Princess*, its sail as flat as a collapsed tipi cover, inched its way into the turn.

Some of the children dropped their toy bows and willow-branch shields, fleeing back toward the huge makeshift camp. Others just stood staring, their mouths dropping open in surprise as the huge keelboat loomed closer.

The *Sioux Princess* flew a white truce flag. She was 55 feet long, with shallow sides that sloped inward. These formed a pen for the horses and mules grouped tightly behind a plank cabin amidships. The boat was propelled upstream, depending on conditions, by its 22 oars, by poles thrust against the bottom, by two long ropes called cordelles—or, when fate chose to smile on the overworked crew, by a square sail filled with favoring wind.

But today there was no favoring wind. The river was too narrow at this point for proper use of the oars, the bottom too uneven for easy poling. So the mostly Creole French crew, hired on in New Orleans, manned the cordelles from either bank. Laboriously, muscles straining, they tugged the heavily laden boat against the current.

Wes Munro, a thin, hard-knit, rawboned man with the butts of two British dueling pistols protruding from his sash, stood in the prow. His face was clean-shaven, his collar-length salt-and-pepper hair clean and evenly trimmed, his linsey clothing immaculate. But his eyes—as flat and hard as two chips of obsidian—belied his genteel appearance.

His hands were folded atop a one-pounder cannon. Spaced at regular intervals around the rest of the heavily armed boat were swivel-mounted flintlocks that fired eight-ounce balls.

"Heave into it, you frog bastards!" shouted a

man behind Munro, calling out across the river to
the crew on the banks straining over the cordelles.
"You pack of spineless city squaws, *heave!*"

Hays Jackson lowered his voice and said to
Munro, "Must be a big powwow. Christ, look how
many red devils! This ain't no reg'lar summer camp
marked out on the map."

Jackson was thickset, short, but built like a nail
keg. His small eyes were set too close together. A
nervous tic kept his left eye perpetually winking at
whomever he spoke to.

Munro nodded as he waved to the children who
still remained, curiously staring.

"Whatever's going on, it's no war council. We
need replacements for those three men we lost in
the Mandan raid. Time to announce our arrival."

The one-pounder was always kept loaded with
black powder. Munro removed a flint and steel
from the possibles bag on his sash and sparked the
touch hole. A moment later the cannon exploded,
belching black smoke and smoldering wadding. Its
cracking boom echoed out over the calm river.

With terrified screams, the remaining children
dropped their toy weapons and raced up the bank
toward the safety of their people.

Hays Jackson threw back his head and laughed.
His few remaining teeth were stained brown from
tobacco. "Lookit them little red niggers scatter!"

Then he shouted out to the crew, "Snub the
ropes to them cottonwoods, you raggedy-assed
Pope worshippers!"

"Good thing they don't palaver much English,"
said Munro, "or they'd have opened your throat by
now."

"Them lubbers?" Jackson hawked up a wad of
phlegm and spat it overboard. "They wouldn't say

boo to a goose, the white-livered cowards. You seen what a pack of wimmen they was when the Mandan hit us. Why, even that old codger we hired on at Bighorn Falls has got better oysters on him!"

At the booming roar of the cannon, the riotous camp had fallen silent. The Indians were more curious than afraid. Since the Fort Laramie accord seven winters ago, in the year the whites called 1851, keelboats had become a common sight in the Wyoming Territory. That crucial 1851 council had guaranteed the Cheyenne and Arapaho a broad tract of land that stretched from western Kansas to the toes of the Colorado Rockies. But it had also granted to the palefaces unrestricted transit rights across the territory.

Touch the Sky was among the first braves to reach the water. He noticed the two white men on deck, the drunken Creoles scattered along the banks, the horses and mules clustered in their shallow pen.

Then his eyes met those of a bearded old man standing amongst the animals. He was dressed in buckskin shirt and trousers with a slouch beaver hat.

A shock of recognition made Touch the Sky smile wide: It was his friend Old Knobby, the hostler from Bighorn Falls! Touch the Sky had been his friend back in the days when the Cheyenne youth was called Matthew Hanchon and lived among the whites.

"Knobby!" he called out, racing closer to the river.

Then he drew up short, confused and troubled.

Old Knobby had clearly recognized him. But now he made a quick, desperate gesture toward the other two white men, warning the youth with his eyes to stay quiet and pretend they were strangers to each other.

Then Old Knobby deliberately turned his back on his former friend, and Touch the Sky realized that trouble was in the wind.

Chapter 2

Old Knobby watched, hidden amongst the horses in his charge, as Hays Jackson barked out orders to the crew, mixing English with bad French. Crates were ripped open and merchandise heaped on the deck: gaudy military-surplus medals, bright beads, blankets, mirrors, sugar, coffee, tobacco, powder and ball and gun patches.

Knobby had been as surprised as the Cheyenne youth when he recognized his young friend Matthew Hanchon—Touch the Sky, the former mountain man remembered now. For Matthew's friend Corey Robinson had told him the youth's new Cheyenne name. But Knobby had seen enough, since beginning this ill-fated journey, to realize that Wes Munro and Hays Jackson spelled serious trouble to the red nations—and to anyone else who tried to block their trail.

After what Knobby had already seen, he sensed

it was a dangerous business to let these ruthless hardcases know that Touch the Sky knew him—or that the youth understood English. The best way to survive around men like this was by not calling attention to yourself.

Knobby had recently closed down his feed stable in Bighorn Falls and hired on as hostler at the mustang spread of John and Sarah Hanchon, Touch the Sky's adoptive white parents. The Hanchon spread was thriving now that their Cheyenne boy had whipped the gunmen Hiram Steele had hired to drive them out.

When Munro and Jackson had sailed into the Wyoming Territory, offering top dollar for good horseflesh for their journey, all had seemed well. Munro had presented credentials identifying him as an official with the United States Indian Department. This was a "goodwill" voyage, Munro had explained, to pour oil on the troubled waters of white man-red man relations.

Munro had offered Knobby a handsome salary to accompany them temporarily as hostler, and John Hanchon had readily agreed—Munro seemed friendly enough, and Hanchon welcomed any attempt to improve life for the Indians, especially now that his adopted son lived among them. Despite the fact that he had been forced to kill several of them in his younger days, Knobby too respected much about the red man and had learned many of their ways.

But then the *Sioux Princess* had anchored at the friendly Arapaho village of Chief Smoke Rising. And Knobby had soon learned that he was working for ruthless murderers who had a secret agenda of their own.

Munro had welcomed Smoke Rising aboard the

keelboat and showered him with gifts. But Knobby, ignored and unobserved, had also seen Munro
trying to convince the old chief to sign some kind
of document. Smoke Rising, who spoke some
English, had remained friendly enough. But he'd
stubbornly refused to sign the "talking paper."

Munro had not pressured the chief. But at a high
sign from his boss, Hays Jackson had accompanied
Smoke Rising ashore. Knobby had followed them
and watched, in the moonlit darkness, as Jackson
easily overpowered the ailing chief and smothered
him to death with his own blanket. Munro had later concluded his mysterious deal with a rebellious
subchief named Red Robe, who affixed his mark
to the document.

Now, as old Knobby watched the braves crowd
together along the shoreline, he realized the
Cheyenne tribe was in trouble too. *All* the Plains
Indians were. Somehow, despite the risk, he had
to meet with Touch the Sky and warn him.

"I bring friendly greetings from the Great White
Council in Washington," said Wes Munro. "These
gifts are to show that the red man is brother to the
white."

Munro spoke in the informal mixture of
Cheyenne and Sioux tongues which was understood by most Plains Indians tribes. He and Chief
Gray Thunder, surrounded by Arrow Keeper and
the clan headmen, stood before the same hide-
covered lodge where the chief-renewal had recently taken place. Gray Thunder had folded his arms
over his bone breastplate to show the white man
he was received in peace.

Touch the Sky, still deeply troubled by Old Knobby's strange behavior, watched from a distance. He

had expected to be called forward to translate. Then he realized this neatly dressed white man spoke the Indian tongue with passable skill.

"Your gifts I welcome on behalf of my tribe. But these are indeed strange words," responded Gray Thunder. "The white man brother to the red? Then is it the white man's way to kill his brothers? To slaughter unarmed women and children in their sleep? To place a bounty on his brothers' scalps? And when the paleface hiders destroy our buffalo herds—is this too brotherly love? I would need to live another lifetime to understand such a cruel and murderous love."

The headmen murmured their approval of these words. Gray Thunder was still a powerful, vigorous warrior, though well past his fortieth winter. Even now, when the clan fires were lit and the clay pipes filled, the young warriors spoke with awe of his exploits against the Crow and Pawnee and Ute.

Nor could Touch the Sky in fairness resent Gray Thunder's coldness toward him. A good chief represented the collective will of his tribe, not his own feelings. Many in the tribe simply did not accept Touch the Sky, though few denied his skill and courage in battle.

"These sad things you speak of," said Munro, "are true enough. But they are the work of only a few whites. Do you stop eating all berries on the bush because a few are rotten? Are there not evil Indians who kill their own and steal from their people? The Great White Council wants peace throughout the land."

"Peace?" said Gray Thunder. "To the hair-faces this is only a word, a thing of smoke! The red nation was once at peace with the white. But peace was not good enough. Those Indians who choose the path of peace are told to stop hunting, to grow gardens like women. They are herded away to barren lands no white man wants. They are forced to dress like whites and pray to the white man's God. Peace is not worth such a price!"

Again the headmen murmured their approval.

"Seven winters ago, in 1851," said Munro, "your great Chief Yellow Bear"—here Munro made the cut-off sign for speaking of the dead, which impressed all the Cheyenne observers—"and many other chiefs signed the talking paper with the Bluecoats at the soldier house called Fort Laramie. That paper promised a vast and permanent territory for your people, a rich and beautiful land. Has the Great White Council east of the river called Great Waters ever tried to steal that land back?"

"No," said Gray Thunder, "certainly not all of it at one blow. But we are like birds who are told, 'You may have this limb, and this limb, for your nest. Only, we will cut down limbs and strip bark all around you.' The paleface hiders destroy our herds, and the Bluecoat pony soldiers build their soldiertowns in the midst of our best hunting grounds."

Munro had already decided this was a bad time to carry out the main part of his scheme. Clearly some huge ceremony was taking place, judging from the finery of the braves and the vast numbers of Indians congregated. Many chiefs could be bribed, but not when they were surrounded by their headmen. He would have to try again later— one way or the other, he would succeed.

Munro was a former "long hunter" from the Cumberland Gap. He could speak smatterings of many Indian tongues, and was familiar with Indian customs. Thus he had proved instrumental in the tricky negotiations which eventually had wrested a veritable nation from the Southeastern tribes.

After helping to swindle the Cherokee, Chickasaw, Choctaw, and Creeks out of their homelands, he had proved his worth to friends in high political places—including Missouri Senator Leigh Hammond, a stump-screamer whose considerable capital was behind this illegal expedition. Now, as Gray Thunder said, the once-proud tribes back East were farming and wearing shoes and answering roll calls like prisoners. And white land speculators had grown wealthy.

So now Munro was following the advice of a popular sentiment of the day: *The sun travels west, and so does opportunity.*

"I have listened carefully to your words," he told Gray Thunder. "I will speak the things you say before the Great White Council in Washington. I respect the red man. And I respect you, Chief Gray Thunder. I have counted the eagle tail feathers in your bonnet."

Gray Thunder's war bonnet trailed nearly to the ground, one feather for each time he had counted coup or slain an enemy.

"Perhaps you do truly respect the red man," Gray Thunder said. "You have troubled yourself to learn our tongue. Few whites do this. Though I fear it can do no good, I am grateful that you will speak for us at the white council. I do not deny that there are some good men among the palefaces. But there are never enough good men to stop the bad.

"Again, on behalf of my people, I thank you for these fine gifts."

Munro had given much away on this trip. But he knew the Indians had given much more. It

had been the same almost everywhere he sailed.
On the Missouri, the Platte, the North Platte,
the Sweetwater, the Yellowstone, the Powder, the
chiefs, or sometimes any brave calling himself a
war leader, had affixed their marks to contracts
which gave up the Indian homelands, millions of
acres, for an annual payment amounting to a few
wagonloads of trinkets.

Munro had felt it coming back in the 1840s. That
was when the expansionists began to argue that
it was absurd for the geographical unity of the
U.S. to be broken up by groups of wild Indians.
At the very least, they argued, the transportation
routes must be cleared—an argument that especially pleased the railroad promoters.

And an argument, Munro knew, which was
indeed true. Travel in the West was hard and
dangerous. Places were god-awful far apart, with
water often scarce. Sand wore out wooden axles,
and green lumber shrank in the dry air. The sympathetic public back East was in an uproar over
the terrible sufferings of the "handcart Mormons"
and the immigrants who'd died by the hundreds in
the massacre at the grassy swale called Mountain
Meadows.

Now public sentiment called for a transconti-
nental wagon road first, to be followed by a
railroad if the wagon road proved itself. And
Senator Hammond already knew the proposed
route, thanks to insiders on the key Congressio-
nal committee. It would follow the Platte Valley-
South Pass-Humboldt River route, right through
the heart of Plains Indian homelands.

And even if the railway plan failed, Senator
Hammond was behind the not-yet-passed Home-
stead Act. This would grant 160 acres of Western

land to settlers at $1.25 per acre—and Munro planned to own many of the best land parcels, Indians be damned.

"Gray Thunder," he said, "I have one request. Several sleeps ago, while my crew was freeing our boat from a sandbar on the Platte, we were raided by Mandan renegades. Three of my men were killed. I need replacements to man the poles and oars, the towing ropes.

"If you will loan me three of your strong young bucks to complete our journey, I will pay your tribe handsomely in new guns and ammunition. They will be gone perhaps for the duration of two or three moons. Then they will return to your tribe when my boat sails back to the St. Louis settlements."

Gray Thunder listened in silence, his face impassive. "I have no authority to grant or deny your request until I have spoken of this matter at council. I will speak with my headmen at the Council of Forty. However, I do not think they will approve such a plan. It is not the Shaiyena way to leave one's tribe. Still, I will give voice to your request. I will also tell the headmen you appear to speak one way to the red man, not with a double tongue."

Munro nodded. "*Ha-ho, ha-ho*," he said in Cheyenne. "I thank you. I will wait aboard my boat for your decision. And I leave an offering to this place."

Munro opened his possibles bag and scattered rich brown tobacco on the ground. These Cheyenne words and gestures further impressed Touch the Sky and the other observers.

But even as Touch the Sky watched Munro return toward the river, a pebble bounced off the Cheyenne's back. Startled, he glanced toward his left.

Old Knobby peered out from behind a gnarled cottonwood, his grizzle-bearded face troubled. He gestured toward Munro, then bent his hand in Indian sign talk for the crooked arrow: the symbol of the liar.

Then Knobby cocked his head back toward a cedar copse behind him. Touch the Sky nodded once, slipping away to meet his old friend.

Chapter 3

"Well, cuss my coup if it ain't young Matthew!" exclaimed the old mountain man when the youth joined him. "Only, I best call you by your Cheyenne moniker now, Touch the Sky. I reckon *this* child never figgered on seein' you agin. You got some growth on you, tadpole, since I last seed you. Collected some battle scars too, by beaver!"

This was a reference to the gnarled mass of burn scar covering Touch the Sky's stomach—a legacy of his long night of torture in the camp of the whiskey trader Henri Lagace. There was also a jagged knife scar high on his chest. This had been inflicted by a white sentry after Wolf Who Hunts Smiling had deliberately alerted him in hopes of seeing Touch the Sky killed.

"I heerd Munro spilling all that chin music jist now about respect for the red man," said Knobby. "Respect. Pah! This hoss'll be ear-marked and hogtied iffen that murdering devil and his partner Hay Jackson ain't lower than snakeshit!"

Quickly, Old Knobby explained everything: that he now worked for John Hanchon and had hired on temporarily to accompany the keelboat crew on their "goodwill" voyage.

"Right from the get-go," said Knobby, "it made this hoss plain oneasy to see them two palaverin' in secret with subchiefs and givin' weapons to raggedy-assed renegade braves. I wanted to pack my possibles and git the hell out. But I figgered they might track me down and do for me. Then I seed with my own eyes when Jackson kilt Chief Smoke Rising pure as gumption. I doan know 'zacly what them two got on the spit. But it means bad cess for the red man."

Touch the Sky had listened with eager joy to the news that his adoptive parents' mustang ranch was now thriving. But the rest of Knobby's report left him full of cold apprehension.

Touch the Sky spoke in English. The words felt odd and stiff on his tongue after all this time without practicing them.

"My only friend among the elders," he said, "is Arrow Keeper, the tribe shaman who protects the Medicine Arrows. I'm his helper now, and we have to be present soon at the Sun Dance ceremony. But I'll go to him now and tell him what you've told me."

Knobby approved this with a nod, removing his slouched beaver hat for a moment to mop the sweat from his forehead. A patch of hideless bone at the top of his skull marked the spot where a Cheyenne warrior had almost raised the mountain man's scalp.

"You do that, sprout. This child best git back

afore he's missed. But jist you mind. That-air
Munro and his queer-blinkin' pard Jackson will
kill a man as casual as you or me'll let daylight
into a prairie chicken. Doan go lookin' for your
own grave!"

Touch the Sky nodded. While Knobby threaded
his way through the trees toward the river, the
youth sought out old Arrow Keeper at his tipi.
The shaman was painting and dressing for the
upcoming ceremony. He had donned his crow-
feather war bonnet and his magic panther skin
that was said to make Bluecoat bullets go wide.
It was decorated with porcupine quills, feathers,
leather fringes, and hair from enemy scalps.

The shaman frowned when he saw that Touch
the Sky was not yet painted or dressed.

"Little brother, have you eaten strong mush-
rooms? The Sun Dance begins soon and you still
wear your clout and leggings. You are one of the
Dance Priests."

"I know, Father. But I would speak with you first
before I dress."

"I have ears for your words. Speak them."

Touch the Sky repeated everything Old Knobby
had told him. While he spoke, the cracked-leather
seams in Arrow Keeper's face deepened.

"A word-bringer recently arrived from Smoke
Rising's camp with word of his death," said Arrow
Keeper. "There was no sign of violence, and his
tribe assumed the old man had simply tired of life
and given up his spirit to Maiyun. If, as your paleface friend claims, he was smothered, this could
have been done without marks. Now their acting
chief is Red Robe."

Arrow Keeper was deeply troubled by Touch
the Sky's report. There would be no reason for

the white who spoke these things to be lying, and Red Robe was a notorious hothead who ruled by intimidation more than respect. It all made sense.

For a moment his eyes cut to the coyote-fur pouch resting atop his buffalo robes, as if drawing strength from it. Touch the Sky followed his glance. He knew that pouch held the four sacred Medicine Arrows. For these was Arrow Keeper named, in honor of his important mission to protect the four arrows with his very life, to keep them forever sweet and clean. The fate of the Medicine Arrows was the fate of the entire tribe. If the Arrows were sullied, the tribe was sullied; if they were lost, the tribe was lost.

And Touch the Sky knew that some day, when Arrow Keeper crossed over to the Land of Ghosts, the task of protecting the sacred arrows would pass on to him.

"Little brother, this man Munro seemed straight-arrow. He seemed to speak one way to Gray Thunder. Do you trust this white man named Knobby?"

Without hesitating, Touch the Sky nodded. "With my life. He has many winters behind him, Father, but his brain is strong and clear like yours. He is brave and true. Though he has fought and killed red men in his youth, he respects them. And he once saved my life when a Bluecoat officer meant to draw his weapon and shoot me."

Arrow Keeper nodded, his red-rimmed eyes pouchy with weariness. "Go now and prepare for the Sun Dance. Quickly. I will speak with Gray Thunder. But I fear the tribe is in grave danger. Last night, in a medicine dream, I saw blood on the Sacred Arrows!"

*   *   *

This season, as it was every ten years, the annual Sun Dance was combined with the chief-renewal dance, making it an especially important and grand occasion.

Arrow Keeper had carefully explained to Touch the Sky that the Sun Dance was not only to welcome the coming of the warm moons—it was also the Cheyenne tribute to their ponies, the most important element of their survival as Plains warriors. Today a newborn pony, the "gift horse," would be dedicated to Maiyun, the Good Supernatural.

Touch the Sky had been with the tribe long enough to attend two Sun Dances. But now Arrow Keeper was training him in the shaman arts, and this was his first occasion as a Sun Dance Priest. His nervousness was so great that, for the time being, the new danger Knobby spoke of was pushed to the back of his thoughts.

The drummers had begun late that morning, beating out a steady rhythm on hollow logs with their stone war clubs. Touch the Sky had donned his war bonnet, his new mountain-lion skin, and his best quilled and beaded moccasins. He had painted his face as if for battle: his forehead yellow, his nose red, his chin black. He had tied bright pieces of red cloth into his long, loose black locks.

Touch the Sky had carefully rehearsed his part with Arrow Keeper. Nonetheless, beads of nervous sweat felt like lice crawling through his scalp as all eyes turned upon him and old Arrow Keeper when they marched into the center of the camp clearing.

"Bring out the gift horse!" Arrow Keeper shouted in his gravelly but powerful voice, officially opening the ceremony.

This honor fell to Honey Eater as the daughter of their departed chief, Yellow Bear. Dressed in her finest doeskin dress, one adorned with shells and stones and gold coins for buttons, she led the bandy-legged roan colt into the center of the clearing by its buffalo-hair bridle.

Despite his nervousness, Touch the Sky was struck by Honey Eater's frail beauty—her magnificent black hair was braided in fresh white columbine. The high, prominent cheekbones were so perfect they might have been sculpted by the finest artist on the Plains. The long, thick eyelashes curved sweetly against them when she closed her eyes.

Arrow Keeper staked the gift horse in the exact center of the camp circle. Then Touch the Sky measured off ten paces from the pony—one pace for each of the ten main Cheyenne bands. Then he knelt and made a fire. When the flames leaped high like dancing spear tips, he lay four pieces of calico radiating out from the fire in the four cardinal directions of the wind.

At a word from Arrow Keeper, Honey Eater began the actual dance by singing a holy song. Her sweet, clear voice rang out with the purity of fine crystal. By the time she finished, a captivated hush had fallen over the entire camp. The air seemed to fairly spark with expectation.

Now, by custom, it was Arrow Keeper's task to call forth a lone brave to dance first by himself— one who had proven his bravery many times.

"Black Elk!" he shouted. "Begin the dance!"

The young war chief, fiercely magnificent in his full battle rig, stepped forth. First he and Arrow Keeper smoked the holy medicine pipe, lit only for this occasion. The drummers picked up their tempo and chanted *"Hi-ya hi-ya!"*—the Cheyenne war cry—over and over in a sing-song cadence. Black Elk danced in an ever-tightening circle around the gift horse, kicking his feet high and chanting with the drummers.

Black Elk finished his solo dance. Then, as the Dance Law required, he made a public recitation of all his coups in battle. When the war leader had finished describing his heroism, he turned toward their new peace chief and solemnly proclaimed the ritual words:

"Gray Thunder! As I have done it, so must you protect the people!"

Now, for the first time, the entire tribe raised a shrill cry of praise and began to dance together as one.

Touch the Sky heaved a great sigh of relief. His official duties as a Dance Priest were over. Now he was free to dance and rejoice with the others. The powerful and solemn ceremony had filled him with awe and drawn him close to the rest. He experienced a rare feeling of harmony, of oneness with the tribe. And when he smiled and nodded to his fellow Cheyenne, they smiled and nodded back.

Today, at least, he belonged!

But his new sensation of joy was fleeting.

During the course of the dance, purely by chance, he and Honey Eater were jostled close together by other dancers. This was the first time in a long while that they had found themselves so physically close to one another.

He stopped dancing, staring into the bottomless dark purity of her huge, wing-shaped eyes.

She too stopped dancing, matching his rapt gaze.

For a moment there was nothing else: no rhythmic drumming, no sing-song cadence of the dancers, only the two of them, locked in their forbidden love. Inside Touch the Sky, it was as if a dam had burst, and all the old feelings of love and desire burst forth, overwhelming him.

An iron grip like eagle talons fell on his shoulder, jolting him back to harsh reality.

He turned his head to confront the enraged, glowering face of Black Elk, who had witnessed their intimate moment of communion.

Quickly, Honey Eater spun away, resuming her high-kicking dance steps. But it was too late to palliate her husband's jealous rage.

"I have words for you, buck—now! Meet your war chief down by the river!"

Chapter 4

The dancers paid scant attention when the two young Cheyenne braves made their way through the crowded clearing. Black Elk remained several paces ahead of Touch the Sky as they reached the line of cottonwoods separating the clearing from the placid river.

Black Elk took care to avoid the anchored keelboat, aiming toward a thicket just beyond a sharp dogleg bend in the river. Only when the two Cheyenne were alone, safe from all prying eyes and ears, did the war leader face his subordinate and speak.

"Would you steal my ponies?" he demanded.

Confusion clouded Touch the Sky's dark eyes. "What does Black Elk mean by this odd question?"

"He means to be answered, Cheyenne! Would you steal my ponies?"

36

"You know I would not."

"Good. And would you steal my blankets, my buffalo robes?"

"Better to ask if a wolf would sleep with a rabbit! I cannot place these words in my sash."

Black Elk's eyes snapped sparks. His leathery hunk of sewn-on ear made him seem especially fierce. "Soon enough I will speak words you may carry off with you. But now, answer me. Would you steal my blankets and robes?"

"Not even if I were freezing!"

"And my meat racks, would you steal from them if you were starving?"

"I would not."

Black Elk nodded. "I believe you speak the straight word. I believe you would never steal these things. Yet you would steal my squaw from me, and do it in front of my face!"

"This is strong-mushroom talk. I would steal *nothing* that belongs to you—or any other member of my tribe."

"You lie like a hairy-faced Bluecoat, Touch the Sky! Just now, I saw how your eyes coveted Honey Eater. Why, the Bowstring Soldiers who enforce the Dance Law might have punished you had they seen you stop dancing without leaving the clearing first. You know this is not permitted, yet you were so full of thoughts for Honey Eater, your brain became tangled!"

"*She* stopped dancing too!"

As soon as he spoke the defiant words, Touch the Sky regretted them. Hot blood flowed into Black Elk's face, flushing his clay-colored skin even darker.

"Yes, she stopped too. Arrow Keeper is right to see the shaman's power in you. Long have you held her in your spell and charmed her as a snake might charm a bird."

"No! I—"

"Your war chief is still speaking, be silent! I do not completely blame Honey Eater. She is a woman, and women are weak in matters of the heart. This is why our unmarried maidens wear knotted ropes below their waist to protect them from the rut. It is the man's job to be strong, to do the right and honorable thing according to our Cheyenne way.

"*You* are the culprit, Touch the Sky! It is you who plays the fox, you who beguiles her. The cow only receives—it is the bull who mounts and penetrates."

Now anger began to kindle in Touch the Sky's keen eyes. "This talk of rutting and bulls mounting dishonors both myself *and* your good, chaste wife. Neither I nor Honey Eater have given you cause to speak so recklessly."

"Would you swear this thing?"

"Gladly, if only for Honey Eater's sake."

"Wait here," said Black Elk.

In a moment he was gone, disappearing rapidly beyond the thicket. Before long he returned. Now he carried a smoothly finished flap of doeskin. Four arrows had been drawn on it with claybank paint, two rising vertically and two more crossing them horizontally.

"You know what these represent?" said Black Elk.

Touch the Sky nodded.

"These are the Sacred Arrows. Swearing on this painting is no different than swearing on the Arrows themselves. I will say this much for you, tall warrior. On matters not concerning Honey Eater, you have always spoken one way, the straight way. I do not believe you would speak in a wolf bark while your hand is on these."

"You are right, I would not."

"Then touch them now and swear this, that you have *never* held Honey Eater in your blanket for love talk since she became my bride."

Without hesitating even the space of an eyeblink, Touch the Sky did so.

For a moment, some of the clouds seemed to clear from Black Elk's brow. But when Touch the Sky started to remove his hand, Black Elk grabbed it and held it in place.

"We have not had done yet. Swear *this* thing too, that you will *never* hold her in your blanket so long as you live."

These words caught Touch the Sky by surprise. Black Elk's strong grip trapped his hand in place. The two warriors faced off for the space of several heartbeats, their eyes locked in mutual challenge.

How, Touch the Sky agonized, could he ever swear such a thing? Had he not placed a rock in front of his tipi, swearing to Honey Eater that his love would melt only when that rock too melted? More important—did she not steal away alone each day to check that rock, to make sure it had not melted? Though Cheyenne law and the weight of tribal opinion opposed their love, it was a true and eternal love. And true love kept itself alive by feeding on one thing only—hope. Hope that somehow, some way, against all odds, the lovers would someday be together.

Chief Yellow Bear's prophetic words, spoken from the Land of Ghosts during Touch the Sky's powerful vision at Medicine Lake, echoed again in his mind: *I have seen you bounce your son on your knee, and I have seen you shed blood defending that son and his mother.*

His mother . . . he had no proof she would be Honey Eater. But neither did he have proof she would not be.

With a sudden surge of strength that surprised Black Elk, Touch the Sky tore his hand away. Now the blood of anger filmed the younger warrior's eyes. His mouth was a determined slit.

"Never! Black Elk asks too much. I have sworn that his bride has been faithful, that I have respected his marriage vows. I will swear to nothing else."

Black Elk's rage was instant. A huge vein in the side of his neck swelled with angry blood. In a moment his bone-handle knife was in his hand.

"You squaw-stealing dog! Now swear with your blade!"

Touch the Sky leaped back, at the same time drawing his lethally honed obsidian knife from its sheath.

"I would never stain the Sacred Arrows by being the first to draw Cheyenne blood," he told Black Elk. "But I have seen how sick jealousy has ruined Black Elk's manly goodness. There was a time when, though covered with hard bark, you were always fair and just.

"Then, when I journeyed to Medicine Lake, you gave in to your jealous, diseased fancies. You sent your cousin and Swift Canoe to murder me in cold blood! This was the act of a coward, not a warrior. Now I will defend myself as any warrior must. Come at me, then, I am for you! This day one of us goes under!"

With a snarl like an infuriated wildcat, Black Elk leaped at him. Touch the Sky used his war chief's own momentum against him, dropping quickly

onto his back and lifting his feet to catch Black
Elk's stomach. He continued rolling back as he
heaved mightily, sending the older brave crashing
into the brush behind them.

In an instant Touch the Sky was back on his feet.
He had time, before Black Elk recovered, to plunge
his knife home. But the taboo against drawing
Cheyenne blood was powerful. The putrid stink
of the murderer would cling to him for life. Even
if the Headmen ruled his action self-defense, never
could his lips again touch the common pipe, his
hands hold a utensil used by others. And never
could he be a shaman—anyone killing a fellow
Cheyenne, even by accident, was forbidden from
taking part in the Renewal of the Medicine Arrows
or any of the other ceremonies.

All of this whirled through his mind in a heartbeat. Again he moved back instead of closing for
the kill. And now Black Elk was on his feet again,
his face still distorted with murderous hate.

"Look at you!" said Touch the Sky. "When I
joined the tribe, how often was I mocked for letting
my feelings show in my face? How many times was
I called Woman Face? And now it is my war chief
who lets his feelings distort his countenance! Do I
follow a double-tongued war leader?"

Touch the Sky did not speak in a taunt, but in a
plea to Black Elk's better self—the better self who
had recently recounted his coups before the tribe.
And his words were not without effect. Though
he still clutched his weapon, chest heaving like
an enraged bull's, Black Elk pulled up short in
his next lunge.

"We have enemies enough outside our tribe for
a lifetime," said Touch the Sky. "Do not sully the
Arrows!"

Before either buck could speak another word, the unseen camp crier's voice rang out above the rhythmic hubbub of the dancing.

"Black Elk! Touch the Sky! Report at once to the lodge of your chief!"

Chapter 5

For a moment Touch the Sky wondered if he and Black Elk had been reported by the Bowstring Soldiers who enforced the Dance Law. Then he realized the crier had no idea where they were.

His sudden curiosity was mirrored in Black Elk's eyes.

"Our chief would not summon us during the dance," said Black Elk sullenly, "unless it is an important matter touching on the tribe." He sheathed his knife. "Our personal battle will be settled later."

Neither brave, however, wished to be in the company of the other any more than necessary. Touch the Sky let Black Elk leave first. Then, when his war leader had been swallowed up in the knot of whirling dancers, he followed.

His curiosity only deepened when, upon arriving at Gray Thunder's hide-covered lodge, he discovered Arrow Keeper waiting with the new chief.

"I looked for the two of you myself," said the old shaman, dividing his piercing gaze between the two new arrivals. "But I could not find you among the dancers."

His pointed tone held sharp reproof for both of them. Neither Cheyenne answered, their eyes flying from the elder's.

Gray Thunder, only vaguely aware of the personal conflict between the two bucks, was clearly bothered by some more weighty matter.

"Black Elk," he said, "we have new trouble. You are our battle chief and must be informed. However, after listening to Arrow Keeper's report and advice, I have decided to keep this matter out of Council. I trust the Headmen. But nothing which passes at Council remains secret for long. And this matter must be tucked under your sash."

Quickly, he summed up what Old Knobby had reported about Wes Munro and his partner Hays Jackson. When he described the murder of Chief Smoke Rising, Black Elk went livid with anger— the old Arapaho was a longtime ally of the Shaiyena. Alongside their Cheyenne and Sioux brothers, the Arapaho had courageously driven the murdering Kiowas and Comanche well south of their present homeland.

When Gray Thunder finally looked at Touch the Sky, a certain distance entered the chief's eyes. His tone too was more remote.

"This white beard who told you about these things he saw, does he speak one way?"

"Always, Father. And he has respect for the red man."

"Respect. This is what the other paleface said

oo. Now I am told he is a murdering liar."

Gray Thunder fell silent, musing. He was young or a chief, his thick dark hair only now showing ne first frosted streaks of age.

"I suspected him from his very first words," said Black Elk hotly. "Words coated with honey! Let me ake a few good warriors down to their boat now, nd we will dangle their scalps from our lodge oles!"

"I was once like you," said Gray Thunder. Quicker to sharpen my battle-ax than to parley. But now I would rather look before I wade into eep waters."

"Everyone knows that Gray Thunder has the ourage of a silvertip bear fighting for its cubs," aid Black Elk. "But only think on what happened o the red man east of the Great Waters. They too vere slow to paint their faces against the Long Knives. Indeed, they greeted them with smiles and helped them survive the short white days of the cold moons.

"And now, only look! The Iowas, the Sacs, he Foxes, the once-proud Shawnees on the Meremec—now they crowd into the white man's tinking cities to trade their best furs for strong vater. Now they are so unmanned by drink they no longer remember the Warrior Way or the old cure songs."

Gray Thunder nodded. Black Elk was quick to rise on his hind legs, but this was well spoken.

"All this is true enough, fiery buck. But nothing draws more hairy faces than the murder of their own. This paleface claims enough power to address the Great White Council. I have the welfare of my tribe to consider. If we kill these dogs, a pack far larger may descend on us in wrath.

Should the women and children suffer because
choose the warpath?"

Arrow Keeper approved these words with a siler
nod. Gray Thunder, Touch the Sky realized, had
more realistic grasp of the sheer numbers of th
whites. Black Elk still thought of them as merel
one more tribe, capable of extermination.

Gray Thunder addressed Touch the Sky again.

"We must listen and watch, learn what their pla
is. You understand their tongue. I have decide
to grant the white man's request. He did not li
about the Mandan raid. Word-bringers from th
south have confirmed it. We will loan him thre
capable bucks to help with their journey.

"It will surely be dangerous. If they have kille
Smoke Rising, a great chief, they will not hesitat
to slaughter three young Cheyenne bucks. There
fore, I will send only strong warriors. You will g
with Wolf Who Hunts Smiling and Little Horse
Do you understand the importance of this missio
to the red nation and to your tribe?"

Touch the Sky nodded. "Yes, Father."

"Good. And do you understand that there is n
room for personal battles within the tribe?"

Touch the Sky understood. All in the trib
knew that he and Wolf Who Hunts Smiling wer
enemies. But they were also the best of the younge
warriors.

Again Touch the Sky nodded. "I have ears fo
your warning, Father. My tribe comes first."

Gray Thunder looked at Black Elk.

"Send your cousin and Little Horse to me. I wi
speak the same warning to Wolf Who Hunts Smil
ing. And, without telling them what is in the wind
have your warriors make ready their battle rig:
and keep them ready. This double-tongued whit

man is clever like a fox, and I fear our wise Arrow Keeper is right. The tribe faces great danger!"

Camped just to the west of the Cheyenne's permanent summer camp on the Powder River were their close allies, the Arapaho. Descended from the same ancestors as the Cheyenne, ancestors who had once roamed the wooded lake country of Minnesota until forced west, the Arapaho too were divided into Northern and Southern branches.

The Cheyenne and Arapaho had experienced minor clashes on occasion. But these amounted to family squabbles. They were close enough that the Arapaho, like the friendly Dakota, would receive Cheyenne exiles into their camps with no questions asked—and even let them take Arapaho wives.

The two tribes also looked remarkably similar in face and body type. Which was why the white militiaman named Fargo Danford was not sure, at first, whether the riders approaching his position overlooking a bluff near Roaring Horse Creek were Arapaho or Cheyenne.

Danford adjusted his Army-issue field glasses, squinting for a closer look.

"Durned if them ain't Arapaho," he finally announced to his men. These riders all wore their hair braided, which most Northern Cheyenne braves did only for ceremonies or in old age.

Danford sat astride a big claybank. He wore a flat leather shako hat, his trophy after murdering a Mexican *vaquero* in California. His Colt Navy pistol was tucked into his holster butt forward to accommodate his left-handed cross-draw.

"If them's 'Rapahos," said Heck Nash, the big, balding man on the roan stallion beside him, "that means they're from Smoke Rising's band."

"That it do," said Danford, "that it do. And it also means these red A-rabs has seen their last sunrise. They're breaking white man's law now. This is wagon road right of way. According to that treaty they signed, they're spoze to steer clear of this land."

Nash held a sawed-off scattergun loaded with a double load of buckshot carefully balanced across his saddletree. The riders clustered behind them were also heavily armed.

These "militiamen," and others like them, had been employed by Wes Munro. They were scattered all along the river routes where Munro had entered into private treaties with the various tribes. Technically illegal, these bands were mostly out-of-work miners who had gone bust in California. Many had been riding the outlaw trail for years, on the dodge from the law. But the only law this far out on the frontier was the U.S. Army. And generous payments to the right commanders ensured that the ragtag militia remained mostly unchallenged.

Their job was to enforce the illegal private treaties—treaties most of the Indians understood little, if at all.

One of the militiamen carried a wooden guidon with a white truce flag flying from it. At a nod from Danford, he rode out in front of the group. The others fell in behind him, spurring their mounts to a long trot.

The white truce flag snapped in the breeze. They descended the long bluff in a loose wedge formation. They bore down on the small party of Indians, who had led their ponies to the creek to drink.

"C'mon, boys, let's put paid to it. It's like shootin' at a bird's nest on the ground," said one of them.

"Damn good thing, Tom," another joshed him. "You couldn't hit a bull in the butt with a banjo."

"Real slow and careful-like now, boys," said Danford. "Don't draw any steel until I give the signal. We don't want to spook 'em. Don't give 'em any time to get out of the weather when it comes!"

The small party of five Arapaho braves was hunting fresh game for its tribe. They were led by a brave named Smiles Plenty.

Smiles Plenty, one of the friendliest braves in the tribe, was in an especially joyous mood today. This despite the recent death of Chief Smoke Rising, whom the tribe was still mourning.

On the day before, his son Fleet Deer, who had only 11 winters behind him, had killed his first eagle with his bow and arrow. Proudly, Smiles Plenty had stood in the door of his clan's dance lodge until late that evening, announcing this feat to all who came. Would such a son not be a great warrior?

Smiles Plenty had spotted the paleface riders even before they rode forward to meet the Indians as if to parley. Despite their truce flag, he was wary. He remembered ten winters ago when the hairy-faced fools tore across the country toward the far-off land of the Modoc tribe, the land beyond the sun which the Long Knives called California. In their mad dash for the yellow rocks, they had broken every promise in their talking papers.

Now Smiles Plenty was worried. But it was no use trying to outrun them. Fleeing from whites was an invitation to be shot. Besides, these whites did not seem intent on any serious mischief. They had slowed from a trot to a walk. Now their horses came forward with their heads down, setting their own pace. Nor had any of the whites drawn his weapon.

His braves were armed only with their bows, their lances, and one old muzzle-loader. So fighting was out of the question. Best to parlay and count on his good disposition, his skill as a diplomat, to get them through. He was the tribe's best negotiator, and had kept them off the warpath more than once with no loss of honor.

"Just let your ponies drink," he instructed the rest. "This thing will pass."

When the whites were close enough that he could make out their faces, Smiles Plenty stepped out to meet them.

Smiling the broad, ear-to-ear, toothy smile that had earned him his name, he lifted one hand. He turned it in a slow circle from the back of the hand to the palm, a universal Plains Indian greeting of friendship. Then he folded his arms to show his band was at peace.

The paleface in the silly leather hat seemed to be their chief. He said something in the white tongue. Smiles Plenty stepped closer, shaking his head to let them know he did not understand.

"Game's over, pards," Fargo Danford had said quietly to his companions. "Time to call in the cards."

A heartbeat later the smile was literally blown off of Smiles Plenty's face when Heck Nash emptied the double load of buckshot almost point-blank.

Suddenly, more rifles and short arms spat fire. Before Smiles Plenty's heels had quit scratching the dirt, the other four braves lay dead or dying.

"Lift their scalps, boys," said Danford as he holstered his Navy Colt butt forward. "I'll need somethin' to prove to Munro that we're doing our job."

Chapter 6

Despite the fact that the Cheyenne seldom ate the plentiful trout which the blue-bloused soldiers loved, rivers were essential to their existence. Every major camp, summer or winter, was erected near a river. Yet, not until he became a member of the crew of the *Sioux Princess* did Touch the Sky begin to truly understand the constant dangers and grueling hardships of river life.

Wes Munro had expected disappointing news when Chief Gray Thunder sent a delegation of headmen to his boat. Instead, to his considerable surprise, the new Cheyenne leader agreed to lend him three strong young bucks for the journey.

As a good-faith gesture (and a practical move through such dangerous territory) the Cheyennes were allowed to bring their weapons. Besides their knives in their beaded sheaths and well-honed throwing axes, all three owned good long guns. John Hanchon had given his adopted son and Little Horse their choice of weapons when they rode to Bighorn Falls to help him defeat Hiram Steele's gun-throwers. Touch the Sky had selected a percussion-action Sharps, Little Horse a four-barrel flintlock shotgun with barrels that were rotated by hand.

Wolf Who Hunts Smiling owned a Colt Model 1855 percussion rifle. It had once been Touch the Sky's. But when Wolf Who Hunts Smiling had made the gesture of returning it, after Touch the Sky saved him from Pawnees, the tall Cheyenne had told him to keep it.

Despite this offering, however, the two young Cheyennes were far from friends. Instead, a grudging, temporary peace of sorts had developed between them. Between them was the mutual respect one brave warrior always feels for another, even an enemy.

But both were of opposite temperaments. And Wolf Who Hunts Smiling, who had watched his father cut down by Bluecoat canister shot, would never accept a Cheyenne raised in the white man's world. Especially one who was so clearly his rival in the warrior arts. His ambition to be powerful within the tribe was great, and they both sensed that someday they must clash.

For the moment, however, all three Cheyenne bucks were united against new enemies. First of all was the mysterious Wes Munro, who talked like a red man but lied like a white. There were also the hostile Hays Jackson, the hostile crew of voyageurs or boatmen, and not least formidable of all, the hostile river itself.

Old Knobby carefully avoided any contact with Touch the Sky. He also clearly preferred the com-

pany of his horses and mules over the company of
Hays Jackson or Wes Munro.

They departed almost immediately after the
three youths had reported aboard and stowed their
gear. For the first few hours a strong favoring wind
from the southeast had filled the canvas sail. Only
occasionally were a few of the crew required to
assist the boat through an embarrass, a spot where
floating debris had formed chokepoint, with long
wooden poles.

Then the breeze suddenly died, the square sail
went limp, and the *Sioux Princess* halted all forward progress.

"Man the cordelles, you raggedy-assed lubbers!"
bellowed Hays Jackson, his left eye winking open
and shut from his nervous tic.

The Creoles groaned. The river was too narrow
at this point to fix the long oars into their locks
along the gunnels.

Men scrambled over the gunnels and splashed
ashore on either side. They trailed long, thick
ropes connected to metal rings on both sides of
the prow.

"The hell you blanket asses waitin' for? An invitation from the Queen of England?" demanded
Jackson, glowering at the Cheyennes. They stood
together amidships, curiously watching.

Little Horse did not understand one word,
though the powerfully built paleface's hateful
tone was clear enough. Wolf Who Hunt Smiling
spoke slow English and understood some of this.
Touch the Sky, however, understood every word.
He was grateful that the Cheyenne way had taught
him to hold his face expressionless and not let his
feelings show.

Jackson gestured impatiently. The three bucks

slipped into the river and up onto one of the banks. They took their place on the cordelles and strained with the rest of the crew.

It was slow, agonizing work. Despite their strength and youth, their hands were not thickly callused for such work. By the middle of the first afternoon, Touch the Sky's hands were raw and blistered. Nor were their thin elkskin moccasins designed to dig into the rocky, uneven ground of the banks. Soon their feet were bloody and lacerated from sharp pieces of flint.

The Creoles despised them and the whites, sticking to themselves. Their informal leader was a small but wiry and tough man of about 30 named Etienne. His skin was even darker than the Cheyennes'. He led his fellows in singing strange songs in French, an odd language which, to the Cheyennes, seemed to be thrust forth out of the nose, not the mouth. It was Little Horse who dubbed them the Nose Talkers.

Clearly, one condition of the voyageurs' service was an unlimited supply of alcohol. They began drinking early in the day and remained drunk. They were constantly broaching another keg of rum or whiskey.

Each night the boat anchored and two camps were made, the three Cheyennes on one bank, the Creoles on the other. Wes Munro and Hays Jackson slept in the plank cabin. Knobby slept on deck under the stars, erecting a small canvas awning when it rained.

The boat's lazaret, the storage area under the deck, was well stocked with provisions: dried fruit, jerked beef and venison and buffalo meat, slab bacon, hardtack, coffee. The Nose Talkers caught trout and cooked them in their camp at night, the smell causing the three Cheyennes to wrinkle their faces in disgust. Old Knobby made biscuits each morning. It was the Cheyennes' responsibility to occasionally supplement the fare with fresh game. Rabbits and pheasants were plentiful near the river. Sometimes they even shot them from the boat.

Three sleeps after their departure, Touch the Sky's aching muscles began to condition themselves to the cordelles. But his feet, like those of Little Horse and Wolf Who Hunts Smiling, were still bloody and lacerated. Some of the deeper cuts had even begun to ulcerate.

They tried all the natural remedies which Black Elk and Arrow Keeper had taught them, but none was powerful enough to help much. Old Knobby took pity on the trio of badly limping bucks. One evening when Munro and Jackson were conferring inside the plank cabin, he quickly showed them how to mix river mud with crushed marigold and myrtle leaves, forming a soothing poultice. Slowly their feet began to mend and toughen.

But there was no end of new troubles and hardships.

On the fifth day of their journey, they passed the fork where the headwaters of the Shoshone River joined the Tongue. The current abruptly picked up strength, slowing the *Sioux Princess* almost to a standstill. Suddenly the boat hit a spot where the opaque river water was boiling furiously.

"Sawyer!" shouted Jackson. "Tack around 'er!"

A sawyer was a submerged tree or huge clump of tree limbs. Trapped in the water unseen, they "sawed" back and forth snagging anything that passed over.

The banks on either side were too steep to man

the cordelles, and too many gravel bars made rowing impractical. So the entire crew lined both sides of the keelboat, thrusting their long poles into the river bottom.

"I said tack around!" Jackson raged. "*Heave*, you pack of spineless maggots!"

He constantly carried a knotted-leather whip in his sash. Normally he used it to lash the deck and gunnels, goading the crew to greater effort. But now, as the keelboat balanced on the feather edge of becoming entangled in the sawyer, Jackson brought the whip across the shoulders of one of the Creoles.

Etienne saw this. Touch the Sky, his shoulder and back muscles straining as he manned his pole, watched the crew leader's eyes narrow with hatred when he stared at the white tyrant.

Wolf Who Hunts Smiling too saw this.

"Hear my words," he said in a low tone to his two companions. "We are on a mission for our tribe, and I have orders directly from my chief. But I am no cowering dog like these Nose Talkers. I swear this thing, if that stinking white pig's afterbirth touches me with his whip, I will use his guts for a new bowstring!"

Such talk troubled the other two. The hotheaded Wolf Who Hunts Smiling had been making more and more threats of this nature lately.

"As you say," said Touch the Sky, "we are on a mission for our tribe. Our task is to discover what these whites are really doing on this journey. I hate the filthy dog too. But our personal feelings do not matter. Perhaps later our chance will come. But for now we must remember that we are warriors and will endure anything rather than place our tribe in danger merely to taste revenge."

"Merely?" said Wolf Who Hunts Smiling. "Revenge can be a sweet dish, and I am ready for it *now*."

"You blanket-asses shut your damn gobs and *heave!*" shouted Jackson, his face bloating with rage. "This ain't no time to palaver!"

The Cheyennes fell silent and threw their all behind the poles. Etienne shouted something in French, rallying the voyageurs. Slowly, inch by inch and just in the nick of time, the keelboat slipped sideways and edged around the furiously boiling water.

Wes Munro, who spent much of his time in the cabin poring over papers and charts, tried to be more diplomatic than his abrasive lackey. He never struck members of the crew and seldom even raised his voice. This was not the result of compassion. To him, men were like dogs—sometimes a pat on the head got better results than a kick on the rump.

That night, to reward them for their hard work earlier in avoiding the sawyer, he broke out rations of expensive Scotch whiskey. The Cheyennes refused their share, opting for rich white man's coffee heavily sweetened with raw sugar.

There had not yet been contact with another Indian tribe. Slowly, as the summer days lengthened and the Wyoming sun's heat grew warmer, they made their way north toward hostile Crow Indian country.

The Crow Nation was currently at war with all whites, the result of a cavalry massacre of one of their villages. Munro had no intention of trying to deal with them. Instead, his plan was to acquire land rights all around them, hemming them in. Then he would convince the Army to drive them south to Kiowa and Comanche country as they had once before.

Soon, as the *Sioux Princess* drew closer to the Yellowstone River, it reached a nearly impassable stretch of water.

At times the Tongue was so clogged with hidden boulders that several oars and poles were snapped. Gravel bars suddenly scraped against the hull with a grinding shriek, forcing the boat to a complete stop. One gravel bar was so long and wide that it took the crew hours to drag the boat free with the cordelles. Other times, thick and well-constructed beaver dams stretched across the entire width of the river, and had to be laboriously torn down after blowing them apart with the cannon.

Once, even Old Knobby was impressed into hard labor, tugging on the cordelles with the others until he coughed up phlegm. Then, ten sleeps after the Cheyennes had departed from their camp, the dreaded confrontation between Hays Jackson and Wolf Who Hunts Smiling took place.

The *Sioux Princess* had cleared a sharp dogleg bend only to encounter the white-churning waters of dangerous, rocky rapids. A narrow and relatively small channel of water skirted the rapids on one side. Only one bank was passable, and half the crew was tugging one cordelle, with the other half poling from the opposite side of the keelboat.

"Tack to starboard!" screamed Jackson. "Tack hard to starboard! Hurry, goddamnit! *Heave* into it!"

In his agitation he made the mistake of singling out Wolf Who Hunts Smiling, who had paused for a moment to get a better grip on his pole.

"Maybe you mistood me, whelp! I said *heave!*"

And then he brought his whip singing smartly across Wolf Who Hunts Smiling's bare back.

The young Cheyenne brave held his face impassive. But his swift-as-minnow eyes blazed with murderous hatred. Quick as a wink, the hot-tempered Cheyenne threw down his pole, whirled around, and seized the knotted whip. One sharp tug, and Jackson was sprawled on the deck.

"You heathen sonofabitch!"

Jackson moved with surprising quickness for such a stout man. In a heartbeat his .36-caliber Paterson Colt pistol was in his hand. But just as quickly, Wolf Who Hunts Smiling's bone-handle knife was raised overhead, ready to be thrown.

Munro happened to be on deck, worried by the rapids. They had not been marked on his navigation charts. As Touch the Sky and Little Horse leaped on their companion, Munro simultaneously caught Jackson's arm.

"Let it alone," he said sharply. "We don't clear that rapids and quick, we'll all be doing the hurt dance!"

Jackson glowered at Wolf Who Hunts Smiling. "Don't miscalculate yourself, Innun. I've scalped better bucks 'n you!"

But Munro had already ordered the Cheyennes back to work. The horses and mules, upset by the turbulent pitching of the keelboat, had quickly become agitated. Old Knobby worked hard to calm and control them.

Again Etienne rallied the Creoles in rapid French. The boiling, churning waters tossed the boat around like a helpless cork in a child's bath. Several crates lashed to the deck broke loose and tumbled into the river, and a buckskin pony leaped over the gunnel in panic.

With a sharp snap, Touch the Sky's pole became wedged between two boulders and broke. At the same moment, one of the Creoles manning the cordelles slipped on the sharp bank and tumbled down into the water, injuring his left leg.

Seeing that the Nose Talker was in no immediate danger of drowning, Touch the Sky leaped into the river, fought his way up the bank, and gripped the thick cordelle in the voyageur's place.

"Heave!" Jackson shouted, fear replacing the surliness in his tone. "Jesus God almighty, *heave!*"

For a moment the *Sioux Princess* balanced between sure destruction and uncertain salvation. Then, like a skittish pony making a sideways little skip, it literally bounced into the narrow, calmer channel.

The heavy boat missed crushing Touch the Sky to death only by inches. But the hapless crew member trapped in the river was not so lucky. His face draining white, he tried to scramble up out of harm's way.

But he was too late. As Touch the Sky watched horrified, the injured Creole was instantly crushed to a human paste against the rocks.

Chapter 7

The *Sioux Princess* survived the rapids with only a few rough gouges to her keel and the loss of some expendable trade goods. But Touch the Sky noticed a change occurring among many of the Creole voyageurs.

The loss of a fourth man on this godforsaken journey was bad enough. But the attitude of their white employers left them noticeably sullen. There was no attempt to recover and bury the remains, no pause for even the simplest of ceremonies. Their comrade's death meant no more to Munro and Jackson than the slaughter of a rabbit.

The Cheyennes were sympathetic. Their tribe placed great importance on recovering the bodies of their dead and preparing them for the final journey. Although the Nose Talkers were an odd lot, and hostile toward the Indians, the three bucks couldn't help feeling a certain brotherhood—were these dark-skinned men, who might have been mistaken for red men if they wore leggings and clouts, not despised by the whites?

On the day after the incident at the rapids, the *Sioux Princess* anchored early so Old Knobby could exercise the horses and graze them in the lush bunchgrass bordering the river.

As a gesture of sympathy toward the voyageurs, Touch the Sky shot a fat mule deer and dressed it out. Assisted by Little Horse, he carried it to the boatmen's night camp and presented it to Etienne. They were limited to sign talk, but the Creole leader understood their purpose. He was not exactly friendly, and did not invite them to visit. But at least he was polite as he thanked them.

Wolf Who Hunts Smiling, however, scorned this gesture.

"These men live in cities and dress as whites," he said when Touch the Sky and Little Horse returned to their camp. "A true Cheyenne does not hunt for lazy, fish-eating drunkards."

The keelboat was visible in the grainy twilight behind them. Fires blazed from the voyageurs' camp on the opposite bank of the river.

"When our chief crossed over," countered Little Horse, automatically making the cut-off sign, "the Lakota Sioux presented our tribe with much antelope meat. It is the red man's way to be generous in a time of sadness."

"Perhaps," said Wolf Who Hunts Smiling. "But the Lakota are our cousins. They raise their battle lances beside ours. Their enemies are our enemies."

"I have ears for this," said Touch the Sky. "But only think, the enemies of the Nose Talkers are also our enemies. Have you not seen how they are treated by the palefaces?"

"So you say, buck. But you too have accepted devil water from the hair-mouth whites, just as these nose-talking fish eaters do. *I* drink nothing of my enemy's except their blood!"

Touch the Sky fell silent, an angry pulse throbbing in his temples. Wolf Who Hunts Smiling had scored a good hit. Once, at the trading post at Red Shale, Touch the Sky *had* drunk strong water with whites who worked for the whiskey trader Henri Lagace. But he had only been tricked into doing so in a desperate attempt to get them to listen to his pleas.

Little Horse could bear no more of this.

"Your tongue is bent double from foolish hatred and jealousy," he said to Wolf Who Hunts Smiling. "You saw how Touch the Sky behaved when those same white dogs held him prisoner in their camp. Did he drink with them then? No! He was prepared to ram an arrow down his own throat rather than cooperate with them."

Wolf Who Hunts Smiling was silent at this. Perhaps he was also recalling the time when Touch the Sky, returning from his vision at Medicine Lake, had bravely saved him from Pawnee marauders—this in spite of the fact that Wolf Who Hunts Smiling had been sent by Black Elk to kill him.

"He was brave," he finally conceded begrudgingly. "He is no coward, certainly. But he also disobeyed his war leader and caused the death of High Forehead by doing so."

Little Horse was about to respond. But Touch the Sky laid a hand on his arm, quieting him. It was no use to argue further with Wolf Who

Hunts Smiling. His mind was stubbornly set, and it was pointless to antagonize him further. Their survival on this dangerous journey would depend on cooperation.

The next day brought a brief respite for the crew. The river widened and deepened as it passed through a verdant valley of hip-deep buffalo grass. A gentle favoring breeze puffed out the square sail.

This gave Touch the Sky an opportunity to do what, so far, he had been too busy to accomplish very often—eavesdrop on the whites as they met in their cabin.

He sat on the plank deck, close enough to the cabin to hear the voices within. He was using a bone awl and buffalo-sinew thread to repair his badly torn moccasins. The cabin had only an open archway for an entrance. But the whites, unaware he knew even one word of English, ignored him as they would a camp dog.

Wes Munro was consulting a U.S. Army map.

"Dakota land," he said to Hays Jackson, "doesn't officially begin until we reach the Whistling Rock fork. So this is still open land. Better put a shack out just in case the Territorial Commission sends out an inspector."

Jackson nodded and whistled to a few of the idling crew. The order was given, and the *Sioux Princess* was moored close to shore.

What followed next was something Touch the Sky had witnessed several times since the voyage began.

With Jackson bellowing out orders, a small wooden shack mounted on wheeled axles was lifted off the keelboat and set ashore. Old Knobby hitched up a team of horses to traces, and the shack was positioned well back from the water. Then the wheels were removed. Fresh white letters on the side of the new pine boards proclaimed THE OVERLAND COMPANY.

Other shacks like it were being knocked together daily by the crew. There was no attention to workmanship. Huge gaps were left between the boards, and they did not even include doors and windows. In addition to setting out the shacks, Jackson used a tomahawk to blaze traces in the area around them.

Touch the Sky had been burning with curiosity about these shacks. Now, as Knobby led his team back up the boarding ramp, the old hostler saw the question in the Cheyenne's eyes.

Knobby glanced carefully around. Then, as he came abreast of the spot where Touch the Sky sat, he squatted as if to examine one of the horse's fetlocks.

"This child has finally got it figgered," he whispered quickly to his friend. "Them piss-ant shacks and the tomahawk claims is mainly to bolster the Overland Company's claim that they're 'proving up' gum'ment land betwixt the reservation lands. Gives 'em a legal claim to it later."

Knobby rose, stiff kneecaps popping, and led the horses back to the shallow pen at the rear of the *Sioux Princess*. Now Touch the Sky listened intently as Jackson's bullhorn voice spoke up.

"You know this Dakota chief?" he asked, his left eye twitching open and closed. "This here Chief Bull Hump?"

"I never palavered with him," said Munro. "But I've heard talk of him."

"Will he make medicine with us?"

Munro was silent for several heartbeats, carefully considering that question.

"From what I've heard, it's not likely. He'll hob-nob with whites, but he won't make medicine," Munro finally replied. "But one way or another, there's a wagon road going up. I've made plans. Old Bull Hump is going to join Smoke Rising in the Happy Hunting Ground."

Jackson grinned. "That shines fine by me. Injuns are nits—and nits make lice."

Now Touch the Sky felt his face drain cold as he finally grasped the gist of Munro's scheme. The heart of the red nations was being stolen out from under the Indians to build a road for the whites!

Absorbed in what he had heard, eager to hear more, he was staring intently through the open doorway when Hays Jackson suddenly met his eye.

Hastily, the Cheyenne looked down and pretended to concentrate on repairing his elkskin moccasins.

But a little nubbin of doubt festered at the back of Jackson's mind. This was several times now that he had caught the tall Cheyenne buck apparently listening.

It could just be curiosity, he told himself. The savage had probably never been around whites before.

Still . . . he sure's hell *acted* guilty.

"Hey, you on the deck," Jackson said to him quietly in English. "Look at me."

But Touch the Sky, nervous sweat making the bone-sliver awl difficult to hold, refused to look up.

Old Knobby was worried.

He hadn't heard the eerie sound in a long time—not since his fur-trapping days in the great mountains he still called the Stonies, though most now called them the Rockies. But he thought he had heard the sound again this morning, when he rolled out of his blankets just as dawn rimmed the eastern horizon in pink light.

The light, fluttering tweet of a bone whistle: the favorite signaling device of the dreaded Crow Crazy Dogs.

Knobby had known the Crow tribe as the Absaroka in the days when they still hunted in the Yellowstone Valley. But as they moved west, encountering more enemies, they became known simply as the Stub-hands. This was a reference to their custom of cutting off their fingers to mourn their dead. Knobby had seen Crow warriors with nothing left but a thumb and a trigger finger.

The Crows were the great thieves of the plains, roaming everywhere in search of booty. And Knobby knew that the Crow Crazy Dogs were the most feared Indian soldier society in the West because they were suicide warriors. Once they entered combat, they were bound by sacred oath—violation of which brought certain shame—to either win or die in the attempt. Joining the Crazy Dogs gave a Crow warrior a special, almost supernatural status—in the eyes of his tribe he was already dead.

Again Old Knobby heard the sound, even closer now: a low, hollow, fluting whistle almost like a whippoorwill. It came from a thicket about 70 yards back from the fog-shrouded river.

Knobby felt his bowels go loose and heavy as his nagging worry turned to sudden fear.

He looked at the one-pounder cannon mounted in the prow, debating. Normally it was fired only in farewells and salutes, though it could also be loaded with up to 16 one-ounce musket balls. It made a hell of a roar, he knew, and would wake everyone instantly.

He was still debating when his favorite horse, a chestnut mare with a white sock on both forelegs, pricked her ears forward toward the thicket. Then Knobby knew for sure.

They were out there.

All hell's soon gonna be a-poppin', he told himself.

As usual, the cannon was loaded with powder, but no musket balls. The old-timer limped forward quickly, tugging at the rawhide drawstring of his possibles bag. He produced a sulphur match and lit it with his fingernail. He held it over the touch hole, and a booming report split the calm silence of dawn.

"What in tarnal *hell*?" Hays Jackson stumbled out of the cabin with his shirt-tails flapping. He clutched a cavalry carbine against his hairy belly. Munro emerged behind him, one of his dueling pistols in each hand.

The three Cheyennes were already racing toward the *Sioux Princess*, their loose black locks flying. The voyageurs, hung over as usual from a late night of revelry, were rising more slowly from their camp.

"You goddamn soft-brained old coot!" said Jackson to Knobby. "The hell are you doing?"

"Stow the chin music," said Knobby grimly as the three Cheyenne bucks raced up the boarding plank. "Best tell your crew to hump it. And break out the spare rifles for 'em. We got Innuns on the warpath."

"Where, you stinking old goat?"

"Over yonder," said Knobby, nodding toward the thicket.

The Crows, the element of surprise already ruined, had decided to attack immediately before the bulk of the crew could form up against them. As if timed for dramatic effect, they charged even as Knobby finished speaking.

With harsh, guttural barks, they streamed out of the thicket on the backs of painted ponies. There were at least two dozen of them. And Knobby knew for a fact now that they were indeed the feared suicide warriors: They wore horse tails gummed into their already long hair, making it trail down below their buttocks. This was the fashion preferred by the Crazy Dogs.

Little Horse too recognized the feared suicide warriors.

"Crazy Dogs!" he shouted to his companions as he raised his scattergun. "*Now* we are in for a battle, brothers!"

The attackers carried no rifles. But their fox-skin quivers were packed tight with new, fire-hardened arrows. They were also armed with their deadly skull-crackers, stone war clubs that could split an enemy's head like a soft melon.

With the suddenness of a prairie storm, arrows began raining into the wooden keelboat all around them. Touch the Sky felt a harsh, fiercely hot stinging in the meat of his right thigh as a flint-tipped arrow found him. He could feel that it had not sunk deep. He ignored it, firing the Sharps and knocking a Crazy Dog off of his horse.

Another arrow found Hays Jackson's right shoulder, and one pierced Old Knobby's slouch beaver hat. But more Crazy Dogs in the first wave went down as they, or their horses, were dropped by the first volley of fire from the *Sioux Princess*.

However, there was no time to reload or insert fresh primer caps. The attackers were too close and advancing too swiftly. Already one warrior was charging up the boarding ramp. Touch the Sky drew his knife from its beaded sheath. In the same smooth movement that drew it, he brought his arm back and threw the knife hard into the warrior's chest.

Several fire arrows thwacked into the keelboat, one dangerously close to the powder cache. Old Knobby hustled to put them out.

Munro had emptied both pistols. Now he leaped toward one of the swivel-mounted blunderbusses. The 22-inch barrel had a two-inch flared muzzle which accepted eight-ounce balls. Unlike the prow cannon, these were kept constantly loaded. He fired it, missing his target. But the smoky explosion spooked several of the Crazy Dogs' horses.

One of the Crows had leaped into the river and jumped over the gunnel unnoticed. Now, as he raised his stone skull-cracker to bash Touch the Sky's head in, Old Knobby screamed in English:

"Look to your right flank, tadpole!"

Touch the Sky spun, glimpsed a movement in the corner of his eye, ducked. The club passed so close he felt the wind from it. His battle-ax was already in his hand. Before the Crazy Dog could recover his balance, Touch the Sky shattered his breastbone.

"*Hi-ya!*" screamed Wolf Who Hunts Smiling, rallying his comrades. "*Hi-ya hi-i-i-ya!*"

Now all three Cheyenne braves stood shoulder to shoulder, repelling boarders with their knives, lances, and axes. Old Knobby fired a blunderbuss, and a charging Crow warrior literally lost his head.

The body, carried forward by nerve momentum, took three or four more steps while blood spumed from the severed neck.

The first wave had been broken, but the second was now rushing the boat. Munro was desperately loading the one-pounder with musket balls.

"Where the hell's them white-livered frogs?" bellowed Jackson.

Touch the Sky glanced back at the opposite bank. The Creoles had all gathered behind Etienne, watching the battle in wide-eyed astonishment. They were not afraid, Touch the Sky realized. They simply felt it wasn't their fight.

Etienne's eyes met Touch the Sky's. The Creole leader saw the arrow protruding from his thigh, the streaming blood where a spear had torn a ragged gash in Little Horse's side.

Munro fired the one-pounder, and two Crazy Dogs were turned into stewmeat. This slowed the assault and bought precious time.

The leader of the Nose Talkers abruptly shouted something in French, leaping into the river. With a chorus of answering shouts, his men leaped in behind him. In moments they were scrambling aboard the keelboat and accepting the carbines which Jackson hastily threw out from the cabin.

Chapter 8

Once the voyageurs joined the battle, it was quickly over.

The Crow Crazy Dogs, true to their fanatical oath, died to the last man. Touch the Sky and Hays Jackson had taken arrows, neither serious wounds, and Little Horse would be laid up for a day or two until the wound in his side started to mend. Two of the Creole crew received minor wounds, and one had been seriously hurt. A stray bullet had killed one of the mules.

But despite the sudden ferocity of the attack, no one aboard the *Sioux Princess* had been killed. For two more days the keelboat limped along, again short of crew members while the wounded recovered. The seriously injured boatman, laid out by a Crow war club, would survive but would be useless for any hard labor. These losses, plus the death of the voyageur crushed at the rapids, held the boat to as few as 15 miles a day.

Then favoring winds again sprang up, and the daily distance was more than doubled for a few days.

Munro's mood noticeably improved, and he was generous with rations of good whiskey and coffee. Even Jackson, to whose surly face smiles were total strangers, cursed less at the crew. Under strict orders from Munro, he avoided any further confrontation with Wolf Who Hunts Smiling.

But Jackson and Munro now had reason to keep a close eye on Touch the Sky.

On the night after the attack by the Crazy Dogs, the two men had met in secret inside the plank cabin.

"That tall red nigger palavers English," said Hays Jackson with conviction. "During the fight, did you hear the old codger warn him to look to his right flank? And by God, he looked."

Wes Munro nodded. As usual he was neatly dressed in a clean linsey-cloth shirt and trousers, his face smoothly shaven. His eyes seemed like hard, flat chips of obsidian in the light of the coal-oil lamp. The two men sat at a crude deal table which had been spiked to the deck. A bottle of good liquor gleamed like topaz among the charts spread out between them.

"That would explain," said Munro slowly, thinking out loud, "why Gray Thunder changed his mind. They wanted to send a spy along. But why? Is it just natural suspicion of the white man, or did the chief receive some kind of warning?"

"Well, I kilt Smoke Rising clean," insisted Jackson. "Just like you told me. No marks on him. The old pus-bag was close to death anyhow.

Even if the Cheyenne got wind of him goin' under, why should it make them uneasy about us?"

Munro glanced away, irritated as usual by Jackson's twitching left eye. Munro always tried to stay downwind of the man too. Munro had grown more fastidious since his days as a long hunter, and Jackson always smelled like a whorehouse at low tide.

"It could just be natural suspicion of the white man," Munro suggested again. But then something else occurred to him. "How does the old man know he spoke English?"

Jackson pondered that, his small, close-set eyes staring into the lamplight. "Might be he don't. Might be it was just natch'ral to yell out in the heat of the fight. It don't strike me as too likely that old sot could know him."

Jackson was no great intellect, but Munro nodded agreement.

"It's also possible," said Munro, "that we're wrong about the buck knowing English. The old man yelled loud, and the warning was clear in his tone. The buck might've understood the warning without understanding the exact words."

"That could be," conceded Jackson. "The crew're dumb as dead stumps, but even they'll sometimes hop when I say 'jump' in English."

Both men wanted to believe that possibility because it was comforting.

"At any rate," said Munro, "we'll keep a close eye on him. We need bodies, and he's a strong worker. But at the first sign he's bamboozling us, kill him."

The three Cheyenne braves had covered most of this Tongue River territory during their warrior training with Black Elk. So when the *Sioux Princess* sailed into view of the Eagle-tail Mountains, their snow-capped tips probing into the blue dome of the sky, they knew they were approaching the Dakota village of Chief Bull Hump.

The Dakota were not such close allies as the Arapaho. But they were on a friendly footing with the Shaiyena nation and had sent generous gifts to the chief-renewal. Once each year a Dakota subchief sat in as an honorary member of the Cheyenne Council of Forty.

So the three Cheyenne braves worried when, once again, the crew began to break open crates of trade goods and heap them on the deck. By now, of course, thanks to what Touch the Sky had overheard, they knew the gist of Munro's plan to steal Indian homelands for the paleface wagon road. Now their attention was concentrated on some plan to interfere with Munro, to disrupt the well-oiled machinery of this engine of destruction.

When and if the opportunity came, they had to get word back to their camp. But now they had a more immediate concern. Chief Bull Hump had been a good friend to their tribe. They wanted desperately to protect him from the fate which had befallen Chief Smoke Rising.

But the keelboat did not stop close to the village of Bull Hump. Munro gave the order to anchor about an hour's hard horseback ride to the south. And the lone brave who was waiting for them there, hiding from his own tribe's scouts and lookouts, was not Chief Bull Hump. It was a rebellious young subchief of 25 winters named Cries Yia Eya.

Cries Yia Eya waited on a buckskin pony. The Dakota tribe did not like riding bareback, but preferred their flat, stuffed buffalo-hide saddles. The powerful young warrior wore a leather shirt adorned with intricate beadwork.

For a moment he glanced with curiosity at the three young Cheyennes. But though they knew him, from brief councils he had held with Black Elk during their warrior training, he did not remember them. He dismissed them with one haughty glance and turned his attention to Munro, greeting him in English.

Touch the Sky had noticed that, since the battle with the Crow Crazy Dogs, Munro and Jackson would not speak around him as openly as before. He was not aware they had heard Old Knobby's shouted warning to him. But a worm of suspicion gnawed at him—the fear that they somehow knew he spoke English.

Munro and Cries Yia Eya disappeared inside the plank cabin. Much later the brave emerged and departed, taking none of the goods heaped on deck.

Munro did not give the order to weigh anchor. Touch the Sky guessed that, whatever was afoot, they were waiting for the cover of darkness— Dakota lookouts must surely surround the area, as all tribes maintained constant security from surprise attack.

Whatever was in the wind, Touch the Sky thought grimly, it could not bode well for Bull Hump. Most of the trade goods on deck consisted of new scatterguns, Hawken rifles, and percussion-cap pistols.

Little Horse too had made a somber inventory of the munitions. He and Touch the Sky were employed in repairing frays in the cordelles while the boat lay idle. Wolf Who Hunts Smiling had been sent ashore by Munro to hunt fresh meat.

"Brother," said Little Horse, "soon comes a storm of trouble. What can we do?"

Frustrated and miserable, Touch the Sky shook his head.

"I wish my medicine were as strong as Arrow Keeper's. Then I might quickly summon magic to help us. Already our shadows grow long behind us. Whatever these dogs have planned, it will happen when our sister the sun has gone to her resting place. Somehow, some way, we must follow them under cover of darkness."

When the Sun Dance ceremony had ended, Gray Thunder's Cheyennes made ready to return north to their permanent summer camp at the fork where the Little Powder joined the Powder.

This operation was impressive in its efficiency. While Black Elk sent scouts out to make sure the route was secure, the women and children broke down the camp. The tipis, which would take much longer to erect than dismantle, came down in minutes. Everything they owned was lashed to travois, along with the very old and the very young incapable of walking or riding ponies.

The warriors formed a double column, the rest of the people traveling between them. Black Elk sent out flankers and point riders. The ponies, well rested and grazed, made good time. In only a few sleeps the summer camp was reestablished along the Powder.

By tradition, each clan pitched its tipis and lodges in the exact spot where they had stood previously. These spots had been carefully marked by buffalo ribs stuck into the earth. A place developed strong medicine that was special to that clan.

The tipis of Little Horse and Wolf Who Hunts Smiling were erected, in their absence, by their clans. However, Touch the Sky had no known blood clan among the Cheyenne. But old Arrow Keeper made sure that two young boys erected the tipi for him on the lone hummock where it had always stood near the shaman's.

Few in camp knew of this new trouble with Wes Munro. They were told only that the three missing braves had been sent to assist the journey. The recent hunts had been good, filling the meat racks with jerked buffalo and ensuring plenty of pemmican for the cold moons. This and the elation following a good Sun Dance left the tribe in unusually high spirits.

However, word of new trouble soon arrived.

On the third sleep after the return to the Powder River camp, River of Winds showed up outside Black Elk's tipi. He was one of the scouts Black Elk had sent out and one of the most trusted warriors in the tribe.

"Black Elk!" he called from outside the elkskin entrance flap. "I would speak with you. It is an urgent matter."

Black Elk lifted the flap and bade him enter. A small cooking fire blazed in a circle of rocks, the smoke curling through the hole at the top of the tipi. Honey Eater sat amidst a pile of buffalo robes at the back of the tipi, finishing a hide on pumice stone.

Despite the obvious importance of River of Winds' message, Cheyenne custom was strong and a visitor always an important thing. Honey Eater prepared hot yarrow tea and bowls of spiced meat for the two men. After they had eaten, Black Elk packed his long clay pipe and both men smoked, speaking of inconsequential matters. Finally Black Elk lay his pipe carefully between them. This was the signal for the serious discussion to begin.

"Brother," said River of Winds, "I did as you told me. I scouted for several sleeps along the Tongue, following the route of the white men's boat.

"Strange little lodges without entrance holes have been erected at places near the river. I cannot read the symbols painted on them in white. Around these lodges, the trees have been blazed with tomahawks.

"More than once I was forced to find cover. Large groups of heavily armed white men are patrolling the area. They are not Bluecoats. I watched one of these groups approach a band of Arapaho hunters near Roaring Horse Creek. Brother, I saw . . ."

Here River of Winds was forced to stop, sudden emotion choking his words off. Honey Eater knew it was important to stay out of the affairs of men. Nonetheless, she stared openly now at their visitor. The hide lay ignored in her lap.

Black Elk noticed this. A fierce frown wrinkled his brow. He knew full well why his bride was so concerned.

"I have ears for your words," he said with impatience to River of Winds. "But I have no medicine to understand them unless you finish speaking them."

"Brother, I saw these hair-faces ride down under a truce flag, as if to parlay with the hunters. Then, with no warning, they slaughtered the Arapahos! They scalped them and mutilated the bodies. They sent them under to an unclean death with no chance to sing their death song—and the leader of the hunters was Smiles Plenty!"

A choked sob escaped from Honey Eater. Even Black Elk, who despised public displays of emotion by men, was stunned into a long silence. Like River of Winds, he too automatically made the cut-off sign. Smiles Plenty was popular among the entire Cheyenne village. Worse, they both knew that by strict Arapaho custom, the names of those who died unclean could never be mentioned again. Their tribal history had ended with their deaths.

Keeping her face averted, Honey Eater suddenly rose and hurried outside. Black Elk watched her, his eyes smoldering with furious jealousy. He realized it wasn't just Smiles Plenty's death that had upset her—clearly, she was fearful for her tall young buck, the squaw-stealing Touch the Sky.

"You have reported this thing to Gray Thunder?"

River of Winds nodded. "He ordered me to report it to you immediately. It will be discussed tomorrow in council."

"These murdering white dogs," said Black Elk, "do they know the palefaces on the boat?"

"I do not know this thing, Black Elk. But they always ride close to the river, and they are thickest everywhere where the boat has been."

After River of Winds had left, Black Elk rose in agitation and paced around the dying fire. This was indeed grim news for the tribe. But something else bothered him, something much more personal—something that pierced him hard in a place where his warrior's armor was useless.

He knew where Honey Eater was right now.

Not wanting to confirm his suspicion, yet driven by some morbid need to know for sure, he slipped out of the tipi. Night had gathered her black cloak over the camp. Fires blazed everywhere, casting eerie shadows. In the clearing at the center of camp, the younger braves were congregating to bet on the nightly pony races.

Keeping to the shadows beyond the fires, Black Elk made his way toward the lone hummock where Touch the Sky's dark, empty tipi stood.

A scud of clouds blew away from the moon, bathing the camp in soft, silver-white light. And there, on her knees before Touch the Sky's tipi, was Honey Eater.

She clutched a smooth, round stone to her breast. In the moonlight limning her pretty face, he could see the glistening tears streaming down.

Bitter bile rose in Black Elk's throat as the words drifted back from the hinterland of memory. Words he had heard Touch the Sky shout to Honey Eater when she and the tall youth were both held prisoner in the camp of Henri Lagace's whiskey sellers:

Honey Eater! Do you know that I love you? Do you know that I have placed a stone in front of my tipi? When that stone melts, so too will my love for you! These white dogs can kill me now, but they will never kill my love for you!

Black Elk's rage was instant.

He rushed forward and seized his wife hard, lifting her from the ground and shaking her.

"What? Are you in rut for your randy buck? For *him* you would gladly get a child in your belly, yet where is *my* son? I will cut off your braids, you unfaithful she-bitch! Then the entire camp will know you are in heat for him!"

Honey Eater was frightened by his terrible wrath. But she was the daughter of a great chief, and her pride was also great. Her own indignant rage was immediate and deep.

"Then cut them off! I am weary of your childish accusations! Do women in rut shed tears? I am worried for him! While you sully the Arrows with this unmanly strong-mushroom talk, *he* faces great danger for his tribe.

"Here! Take this! Cut my braids off now and be done with your threats!"

All Cheyenne women fiercely valued chastity. Thus they carried a "suicide knife" on a thong under their dresses. These were used to kill themselves rather than face rape from captors. Honey Eater pulled it out now.

But already Black Elk regretted his rash outburst. In his overweening pride he would never publicly mark his wife for shame—this would be an admission of his own weakness, a public acknowledgment of his inability to control his squaw.

Roughly, he threw her back down to the ground.

"Then cry for him! Make rivers with your tears, flood the plains. You are wise to do so, for if the whites do not kill him, *I* surely will!"

Chapter 9

Once again unexpected help came to the three Cheyennes in the form of Old Knobby.

Night had descended over the river and, as usual, the braves had pitched their camp on shore. They had been anxiously watching the anchored keelboat since the earlier meeting between Munro and Cries Yia Eya. But they were still without any plans as they waited for the next sign of trouble for Chief Bull Hump's Dakota village. So far all had remained ominously quiet except for the rowdy, drunken singing from across the river at the camp of the Nose Talkers.

"Listen," said Little Horse quietly, "someone approaches our camp!"

A heartbeat later all three youths had slipped back out of the circle of firelight, weapons at the ready. A figure glided closer from the surrounding shadows. Moments later, Old Knobby stood in the eerie orange glow of the fire.

"I swan, you boys faded quicker'n scat!" he said with a chuckle. "This hoss figgered to catch you with your clouts down. C'mon out now 'n' let's parley. There's bad fixin's on the spit."

Touch the Sky spoke briefly to Little Horse, translating this, and they all joined Knobby around the fire.

"I tolt Munro and that pig-eyed Jackson I got the droppin's bad when I et green chokecherries fir breakfast," he explained. "They think that's how's come I'm beddin' down ashore tonight. I doan 'spect it matters much nohow. Them two is too busy layin' big schemes to worry 'bout a toothless old fartsack like Knobby."

Wolf Who Hunts Smiling understood only some of Knobby's talk. Quickly, while Touch the Sky translated for the other two, Knobby explained that he had managed to overhear some of their plans.

In a little over an hour, Munro and Jackson planned to leave the boat with several packhorses loaded with weapons and ammunition. They were meeting Cries Yia Eya at a secret place well back from the river and the rest of the tribe. Several key night sentries for the tribe were in on the plan and would not sound the alarm, though others were loyal to the tribe and would be avoided.

"The pint is," said Knobby, "this Cries Yia Eya is a consequential brave, a real nabob 'mongst the hothead younger warriors. Any way you lay your sights, it's gunna spell trouble for Bull Hump and the rest of the tribe. *This* child doan know the when and the where of it."

Touch the Sky came to the same conclusion Old
Knobby had already reached: Munro and Jackson
would have to be followed tonight. But they were
in unfamiliar terrain and the night was moonless.
And both Munro and Jackson were experienced in
the wilderness—they would carefully cover their
back-trail and could not be too closely followed.

To make matters worse, Knobby now informed
them that some of Munro's militiamen were in
the area.

"Sure as hell's afire," added the old mountain
man, "if they sniff us out, our scalps'll be danglin'
off their coup sticks. We best do some fancy night
scoutin', nazpaw? Doggone my buckskins for ever
signin' on this trip. *This* hoss'll be glad when he's
quits with the whole shitaree."

Touch the Sky was grateful to hear Old Knobby speak of "we." Because of the taboo against
fighting and traveling at night, Cheyenne warriors
did not, unlike the Pawnee, become very proficient
at nighttime scouting and tracking. He and Little
Horse had managed well enough in Bighorn Falls,
when they fought Hiram Steele's thugs. But that
had been on mostly open terrain long familiar to
Touch the Sky. The country surrounding them
now was rife with thick forests, steep cutbanks,
rocky bluffs, and blind cliffs.

Old Knobby wasted no time in giving them their
first lesson.

Near-total darkness like tonight, he explained,
drastically changed appearances and apparent
sizes of objects because details were obliterated.
Rapid, safe movement was impossible unless the
night scout learned to fill the details back in.

He pointed to a nearby tree that rose high into
the sky. It looked much smaller than it would

during daylight, he explained, because the new twigs at the tips of the branches couldn't be seen. Such size and distance miscalculations could be fatal.

Don't look at any one object too long, Knobby cautioned them, and remember that sounds are transmitted a much greater distance at night or in damp air. He also repeated the advice of Arrow Keeper and Black Elk: Smells could be a valuable warning, especially horse smells and the distinctive damp-earth odor from bodies of water.

He instructed them to get their weapons and equipment ready now. He also reminded them to make sure everything was ready and to hand while they were on the move—on a night this black they would have to rely on sense of touch instead of their eyes to find and adjust equipment.

When everything was ready, Knobby called them back to the fire one last time.

"If we get caught out by Munro or his raggedy-assed militia and hafta bust caps," he said, "stay frosty 'n' shoot plumb. Now, this child figgers we got mebbe a hour afore they leave the boat."

They had to prepare, he said, by wrapping their heads in blankets or robes and remaining in total darkness until the whites left. Their pupils would become as big as watermelon seeds and thus gather from the night any stray bit of light.

They did as instructed. As he lay in pitch-black darkness waiting, Touch the Sky listened to the rapid, hollow thump of his heart. His isolated mind naturally turned to thoughts of Honey Eater.

She and the rest of the tribe should have returned to the Powder River camp by now. Some instinct deeper than language told him that right now, at this very moment, she was also thinking of him.

That thought consoled him somewhat whenever he thought about the danger they were about to face. But why did that nagging sixth sense, which Arrow Keeper insisted he must develop as a shaman, also keep painting another picture on his mind's eye: the picture of an angry, jealous, murderously raging Black Elk?

As Knobby had predicted, about an hour later Munro and Jackson led their packhorses away from the *Sioux Princess*.

Knobby made his companions wait another quarter of an hour. Then he and the Cheyennes emerged from their self-imposed total darkness.

"It's only embers now, but doan look at the fire," Knobby cautioned them. "It'll shrink your eyeballs back up."

Touch the Sky was amazed. The clouded sky was completely empty of moon or stars. Yet he could clearly distinguish objects close at hand. Ever farther off, where before he had seen only the black shroud of night, he could distinguish the shapes of trees and hills.

"Write this on your pillow case," Knobby instructed Touch the Sky as they set out. "When you're scouting near enemies at night, never move until you've picked a landmark to aim for first. I know what direction they struck off in. So I'm a-drawin' a bead on that-air stand of pines yonder, see it?"

Touch the Sky nodded and they set out. When they reached the pines, on a bluff beyond the river, Knobby halted them.

"First off, we need to know their gait. Iffen we move too fast, we'll end up on their hinders. Move too slow, they'll meet us on their way home fir breakfast. And this is the safest time to light a match, now that we know they be well ahead of us."

Knobby struck a sulphur match and soon located their tracks.

"Lookit here," he said, grunting as he knelt. "These hoofprints is nigh to overlappin'. That shows them movin' at a walk or a trot. Now a trot's deeper, like these. So we best hump it some."

They made good time at first, Old Knobby always moving them by predetermined bounds between landmarks. The heavily laden packhorses were tearing up divots of earth with their shod hooves. So now and then Knobby simply felt about in the darkness with his hands to make sure they were still on the trail.

After they had been on the move for nearly half an hour, he knelt again to listen to the ground.

"Doan put your ear right on the ground," Old Knobby whispered to him when Touch the Sky too knelt down. "Else you'll hear your own heart a-pumpin', not the horses. Put it *close* to the ground."

Faintly, like a weak, slow drumbeat, Touch the Sky picked up the sound of iron-clad hooves.

"We're nigh onto 'em," cautioned Knobby. "Slow down. Wait till there's natural sounds like the wind to cover our movement."

Soon the sound of nickering horses ahead was carried to them on the wind. The four of them were moving up out of a long draw. Touch the Sky felt his pulse thudding in his palms as they grew nearer and nearer to some unknown danger.

With Knobby leading, the three youths crawled up a long, rocky slope above the draw. Now they could clearly hear the sound of voices, of impatient horses stamping the ground. They were downwind, so they didn't need to worry about their smell spooking the horses.

Touch the Sky reached the edge of the bluff, and peered over. The sight below made ice run in his veins.

A fire had been built in the lee of a ridge, protected from the wind. Wes Munro and Cries Yia Eya stood beside a huge, flat boulder shaped remarkably like a table. The Cheyennes recognized this spot from their days in warrior training. It was called Council Rock, a place where Dakota headmen often met in outdoor council.

Jackson stood between his boss and Cries Yia Eya, both hands holding a piece of paper flat against the rock. The packhorses were picketed just behind them. Their panniers were still unloaded.

In a ring about the three men, still mounted, was a circle of at least 30 young braves—and the flickering tongues of firelight showed that their faces were painted for battle!

"You understand your end of the deal?" said Munro. Cries Yia Eya had learned some English during the year he'd spent as a guide for the Northwest Fur Trading Company. "In exchange for these weapons, and another generous payment every year, the Dakota tribe agrees to surrender rights to a tract of land that stretches from here . . ."

Munro pulled a second sheet of paper out from under the first and pointed. "From here, at the juncture of the Tongue and Medicine Creek, to here at the foothills of the Red Shale Mountains. You agree that your tribe will not hunt nor roam over this territory so long as this treaty is in effect."

Urgently, Wolf Who Hunts Smiling nudged Touch the Sky. According to the Fort Laramie accord of 1851, the tract which Munro had just described ran through the heart of a great buffalo range owned jointly by the Sioux, the Arapaho, the Dakota, and the Cheyenne.

Below, Cries Yia Eya nodded impatiently.

"You also understand," said Munro, "that you are acting as the legal agent for your tribe? Meaning, of course, that Bull Hump will either have to be in agreement with you or somehow removed from leadership?"

"Cries Yia Eya knows full well what the talking paper means," said the bold warrior, his beadwork shirt glittering in the firelight. "He does not mince around the truth like a pony avoiding a snake. This paper is nothing. Give me and my braves our guns *now* and Bull Hump crosses over this very night!"

Munro nodded and Jackson grinned. Cries Yia Eya affixed his mark to the private treaty.

"My militiamen are waiting back near the river," said Munro. "It's best if you take care of this yourself. But if the fight goes bad for you, send a word-bringer back to my boat. I'll signal with the cannon, and my boys will give you a hand."

"The fight will not go bad," Cries Yia Eya assured him. "Even now you are looking at the best warriors in the tribe. The rest are loyal to Bull Hump. They would rather dig turnips with the squaws than tread the warpath with men. Tonight Cries Yia Eya takes over his people!"

"All right, *Chief*," said Munro, nodding with satisfaction. "First let's break out the weapons and make sure your braves know how they operate. Then the next move is yours."

Chapter 10

Knobby and the three Cheyennes had seen and heard enough. At a high sign from the old man, they quickly retreated down the bluff. They hid inside a jagged erosion gully to counsel.

Wolf Who Hunts Smiling's grim face showed clearly that he had understood the slow, clearly spoken English. Touch the Sky quickly filled Little Horse in on the treachery afoot, though the sturdy little brave had guessed enough without words.

"What do we do?" Touch the Sky asked Knobby, despair clear in his tone. "Bull Hump's village is still well downriver from here. We'll never get there on foot in time to warn them."

"Simmer down, sprout," said Knobby. "If we hump it, there's more time than you kallate. This hoss helped load them weapons. The pistols is all brand-spankin' new Remingtons that was broke down for shipping. They got to be put together agin. Them Innuns ain't never seed that model 'n' won't know sic 'em about the mechanism. Munro'll hafta learn 'em how they work.

"Plus, the whole shitaree—the rifles too—is packed thick in oil to protect the workin's from rust on the river. All that gun oil will hafta be cleaned off the firing pins 'n' loading gates afore them irons will crack caps."

Knobby's calm voice had its effect on Touch the Sky. He too calmed down and began to think more clearly. He continued speaking in English to Knobby.

"We won't have to worry about noise, so we can make good time back to the boat. You've got the horses grazing near the river. We can cut out three fast ponies and ride hard to the camp and warn Bull Hump. We *might* be able to beat the others."

"That's the gait!" said Knobby approvingly. "Now you're roarin' like a he-bear Cheyenne. This hoss by God wishes he could ride with you. But there'll be trouble a-plenty as it is, comin' up on a red village at night. Ye doan need no hair-face to draw down fire from the sentries.

" 'Sides, the rheumatic has already got this old bag o' bones stiff 'n' tied up. A hard ride'll crack his tailbone. C'mon, pards—time to make tracks back to the river!"

The three Cheyennes read it as a good omen— at least for now—when a full ivory moon suddenly emerged from the boiling mass of dark clouds. With the silver-white moonlight aiding them, they made the trip back to the river in good time.

Knobby cut a sorrel, a paint, and his favorite, the chestnut mare, from the ponies grazing the bunchgrass in a temporary rope corral. There were leather saddles aboard the *Sioux Princess*. But the three Cheyennes settled for bridles and reins.

Wolf Who Hunts Smiling and Little Horse had used only buffalo-hair hackamores. Old Knobby had to show them how to slip the iron bits into the horses' mouths. Though they said nothing, Touch the Sky could tell they were thinking the same thing—this was yet one more proof of the white man's barbarous treatment of horses.

As they were about to set out, Touch the Sky ready to mount the chestnut, Old Knobby caught hold of his arm.

"Might be that your trail will cross with the others afore you git to Bull Hump's camp. Or mebbe you'll be caught in the lead when the renegades show up. So poke this last bit o' advice into your sash.

"Like I said, that-air Cries Yia Eya is a mighty consequential brave. You knock the wind out o' *his* sail, the whole fleet is dead in the water—you catch my drift?"

The younger braves following the rebellious subchief drew their reckless courage from his example. If Cries Yia Eya were taken out of the picture, the others would have no leader in their traitorous uprising. Touch the Sky considered this a fatal weakness of the red man's warrior code. He secretly believed that red men needed to be more like the Bluecoats on this point—white soldiers rigorously maintained a strict chain of command to ensure a leader in battle at all times, even if the original commander was killed or wounded. But when Indians lost a battle chief, too often they were quickly thereafter defeated.

Touch the Sky nodded. "I catch your drift. Thanks, Knobby."

The hostler slapped him on the back. "Doan forget Munro's gun-throwing militia is in this neck o' the woods. Keep your powder dry, buck, and give 'em a war face! Good huntin' to all three o' ye!"

Touch the Sky grabbed a handful of shaggy mane and swung up onto the pony, laying his rifle across its withers. Moments later the three braves, assisted by generous moonwash, were racing up the sloping bank of the river toward the open flats.

After so many long days cramped up on the boat, it made their blood sing to be on horseback again. The cool wind lifted their long, loose locks like black streamers, flying as one with the manes of the ponies. Touch the Sky drew strength from the feel of the chestnut's powerful, tightly bunched muscles moving with fluid grace beneath him.

The mare too seemed glad for the hard run after so much inactivity. She responded only reluctantly when Touch the Sky drew in her reins as they neared the final rise overlooking the Dakota camp.

The brief exhilaration of the ride was behind him. Now there was only the worry cankering at him: Would they be in time to do anything useful? Or would Bull Hump be dead, and the camp under command of Cries Yia Eya?

They had already discussed their plan on the return trip to the *Sioux Princess*. Sentries would be ringing the camp, stationed in the encircling belt of cottonwood and pine trees which surrounded the village. Those loyal to Cries Yia Eya would be grouped at the north approach to camp—the route from Council Rock that his band would almost surely be taking. So the three Cheyennes approached now from the south.

It was not a night sentry's main responsibility to fire on intruders, but rather to immediately rouse the tribe to possible danger. Nor, with full moonlight showing the Cheyennes' identity, would Dakota sentries be likely to fire on their allies. Though of course, armed Cheyennes approaching at night were clearly violating normal customs and might well be up to no good. Some rebellious Dog Soldiers of the Southern Cheyennes had been known to sneak this far north on raiding missions. Even tribes normally friendly to each other had learned to be suspicious.

Still, they agreed the best plan was simply to ride boldly up and let the sentries rouse the village—this was exactly what they wanted to do anyway. The next step was to confer, as quickly as possible, with Chief Bull Hump.

Touch the Sky was grateful for the calm silence as they approached. At least the still night air was not yet disturbed by the sounds of attack.

As soon as they topped the last rise, clearly sky-lined now against the full moon, a sentry sounded the Dakota's shrill, yipping alarm.

By the time they were halfway down the rise, iron-shod hooves drum-beating, they heard riders galloping out to intercept them. A party of about a dozen warriors, several still naked but armed, formed a skirmish line to stop them. They had no rifles. But all had already strung an arrow into their green-oak bows.

"Halt there or blood must flow!" commanded one of the warriors. "Why do you approach our camp at night, armed like this for battle? We know you as our friends."

Little Horse, who when he was younger had played with a Dakota child taken in by the tribe, spoke for them. He mixed their words with Cheyenne and Sioux words, knowing most Dakota also understood those two tongues a little.

"Because blood *will* flow, and soon, brothers! We must speak with Bull Hump. Even now the hotheaded Cries Yia Eya bears down on your village, backed by rebellious warriors with blood in their eyes. They met this night with paleface dogs at Council Rock. They have new guns and plan to kill your chief. Some of your sentries are playing the dog for Cries Yia Eya and will not sound the alarm."

His words momentarily stunned the others into silence. Then they conferred rapidly in Dakota. One of them leaped to the ground on all fours and bent his head low, listening.

"The tall stranger speaks straight-arrow," he confirmed. "Riders approach! Many, and rapidly!"

"I will alert Bull Hump and check the tipis," said another, "and see who is missing." He rode quickly back down toward camp.

Still, the remaining sentries were cautious.

"Sadly, we do not find your words about Cries Yia Eya difficult to believe. But you must surrender your weapons before we take you to Bull Hump," said the first brave. "You may speak from two sides of your mouth."

The Cheyennes did not object, knowing this was only a proper precaution. The Dakota braves quickly led them into camp. Dogs, upset by these unfamiliar actions, barked and yowled. Already the women and children and elders were gathering near the river. They were desperately searching out places where they had cached buffalo-hide

rafts. At the first signal, they would ferry across
the river and take to the secret escape routes.

Chief Bull Hump met the new arrivals in front of
his tipi. He was an old man of perhaps 70 winters,
and clearly in ill health. His skin sagged off his
bones like the loose coat of an old hound. He
wore his long white hair parted in the middle and
brushed back behind his ears. But in a defiant
gesture, he had donned his bone breastplate over
his blanket.

Bull Hump spoke the Cheyenne language.
Quickly Little Horse explained the desperate
situation facing his village. Bull Hump's leather-
cracked face showed nothing. But it was clear
from the deep furrow between his eyes that all
of this seemed highly suspicious to him.

"You say you are from Gray Thunder's band?
Then do you know Arrow Keeper?"

It was Touch the Sky who spoke up. "I am his
assistant in the shaman arts, Father. He is training
me to be a medicine man."

Bull Hump leaned close to Touch the Sky,
squinting. Arrow Keeper was the most respected
Cheyenne on all the Plains. If Arrow Keeper had
truly chosen this tall young buck to be his assistant, his honesty would be beyond challenging.

"If you know Arrow Keeper well," said Bull
Hump, "tell me this. What does he always carry
in his medicine bag, besides the totem of his Owl
Clan?"

This question stumped Little Horse and Wolf
Who Hunts Smiling. But Touch the Sky spoke up
without hesitating.

"He always carries his magic bloodstone, Father,
which makes his tracks difficult for his enemies to
find."

Bull Hump nodded once, his face still an impassive mask of cracked leather. But he turned to the sentries, and his next words showed that he was now convinced.

"These brave Cheyenne youths speak with one tongue. Every warrior must make ready his rig for battle, now!"

But more bad news arrived. The sentry who had checked the tipis now rode up.

"Bull Hump, our best fighters are missing! Your cousin Red-tailed Hawk and his party are not due back from the trading post in Red Shale for two more sleeps. The others must be following Cries Yia Eya. We have only a handful of blooded warriors, none with fire sticks."

Now Bull Hump was desperate as he remembered—Red-tailed Hawk and his band of 15 seasoned fighters, all loyal to Bull Hump, had taken travois loaded with beaver pelts to trade for rifles and bullets.

And even now, from the north approach to camp, came the sound of many riders drawing closer.

"Dakota Father," said Touch the Sky, "I ask your pardon for speaking up so boldly. But we are the fighting Cheyenne, and we are keen for this battle! Cries Yia Eya plays the dog for whites who are stealing our homeland along with yours. We have discussed a plan to remove the tip from the lance. Give us ropes, Father. Then form up your warriors around your tipi and wait. If we fail, soon enough the bloody battle will come to you."

Bull Hump had no choice but to place his fate in the hands of these three brave Cheyennes. Perhaps, after all, they had been sent by the Great Spirit for just this purpose. He nodded, ordering one of the sentries to give the young warriors buffalo-hair ropes.

The three braves had followed Knobby's advice in forming their plan. They would use the strategy of the buffalo hunt. Hunters never attacked an entire herd—they isolated part of it from the rest, then closed for the kill.

Now the attackers had nearly gained the final tree-pocked slope which descended into camp from the north end of the village. The Cheyennes raced forward, knowing that every moment counted now. Touch the Sky and Little Horse had successfully used ropes to disrupt an attack on the Hanchon spread at Bighorn Falls. They had decided to try their rope trick once again. They knew that the fiery Cries Yia Eya would be riding in front of his warriors.

They reached a spot where a cottonwood and a scrub pine grew across from each other on opposite sides of the sloping approach. Quickly, Wolf Who Hunts Smiling rode out ahead and took up a position behind another tree with his Colt.

Touch the Sky and Little Horse dismounted and slapped their horses hard on the flanks, scattering them. Then, moving rapidly, they stretched the rope out between them and then each hid behind one of the trees.

They were not a moment too soon. Throwing all caution to the wind, Cries Yia Eya raised a hideous war cry as his powerful buckskin leaped over the top of the rise and plunged down toward the quiet village. The ground thundered and vibrated as the main body poured over the rise behind him.

Cries Yia Eya held his new Hawken under one arm. Touch the Sky and Little Horse waited until the last possible moment. Then Touch the Sky shouted, "*Now,* brother!"

Rapidly, deftly, they snubbed each end of the rope several turns around the trees. This left it almost three feet off the ground. The sure-footed pony saw it and leaped at the last moment. For a heartbeat Touch the Sky's hopes sank—now the village was doomed!

Then one rear hoof snagged hard on the rope, it held, and with incredible speed and force the buckskin crashed muzzle first into the ground.

Cries Yia Eya lost his rifle as he tumbled forward in a fast somersault. He slammed into the ground, stunned. Before he could recover and rise, Touch the Sky had raced out from the right flank. Now he rammed the muzzle of his Sharps into the rebellious subchief's neck. He spoke in Cheyenne, but his meaning was deadly clear.

"One twitch, and you cross over tonight!"

The surprised warriors, following hard upon Cries Yia Eya's heels, reined their ponies hard to avoid trampling him. They flowed past their downed leader like a raging river parting around a huge boulder in midstream. As a brave lifted his rifle to fire at the lone, brazen Cheyenne, a shot rang out from Wolf Who Hunts Smiling's position.

The brave's shield flew from his hand as Wolf Who Hunts Smiling's bullet struck it. The Cheyennes had already agreed to avoid shedding blood after dark—a serious taboo to their tribe—except as a last resort. A second Dakota brave raised his pistol to fire at Touch the Sky.

Now Little Horse fired his scattergun into the trees, the buckshot raising a loud clatter. He quickly rotated all four barrels and fired them in succession. The roar of the shotgun was deafening and spooked several of the Dakota ponies. Deflected buckshot rained down on the warriors and many of them flinched.

By now Wolf Who Hunts Smiling had loaded another primer cap and blown a brave's war bonnet off his head. This unexpected armed resistance, and the capture of their leader, confused the others. Where had the tribe gotten guns, and how many? Rumors suddenly flew through their midst that Red-tailed Hawk and the rest must have returned early with new munitions. Many now believed they were under heavy defensive attack and retreated back over the rise.

"Your war leader is only a bullet away from death!" shouted Little Horse in his odd blend of Dakota and Cheyenne. "Look near the river! Your wives and children and old grandmothers huddle in fear—those whom you are sworn to protect! Even now your old chief stands bravely in front of his tipi, prepared to die like a man. Who among you will shamelessly shed Bull Hump's blood?"

Cries Yia Eya tried to shout out something. But Touch the Sky growled like an angry beast and threw his weight into the rifle. The notched sight pressed into Cries Yia Eya's throat hard enough to choke his words off.

About half the warriors remained, uncertain what to do, wondering if they were surrounded by Cheyennes—certainly no warriors to be trifled with. Then one of them shouted something and pointed down toward camp. The others looked where he pointed and fell silent.

Chief Bull Hump, alone, walked slowly up the slope toward them. Eerie silver moonlight gleamed off his bone breastplate. In the ghostly light the pale, gaunt figure looked almost like a spirit wraith from a medicine vision. Ten paces out from Touch the Sky and the prisoner, he stopped.

"Dakota warriors!" he shouted. "Here stands your chief unarmed, with the yellow leaves of age clinging to the brow where once a dark mane flew as he raced into battle! Kill him, then, and follow Cries Yia Eya! Follow the red traitor who has sold your buffalo ranges for brutal power!

"Kill your chief now, as the women and children watch from the river. *Kill* him! And let he who sends this old warrior under also boast how, like Cries Yia Eya, he played the white man's dog, while young cheyenne strangers fought for the Dakota people!"

These words had a profound effect on the remaining warriors. Their shame now was almost palpable. One after another they lowered their weapons, some dropping them to the ground.

Then, to the last man, they folded their arms in the universal Indian sign for peace, and Touch the Sky knew the immediate crisis was over.

Chapter 11

Fargo Danford sat astride his big claybank on a long ridge overlooking Bull Hump's Dakota village from the south.

In the generous light of the full moon, he had watched the drama unfold below as if he were a spectator in a huge outdoor theater. The action had been exciting enough, he conceded. Damned entertaining, actually. Those three bucks were young, but clearly not the type to rabbit at the first sound of a war whoop.

But Wes Munro was definitely going to be unhappy.

To one side of Danford, Heck Nash sat his saddle on the big roan stallion. The sawed-off scattergun which had destroyed Smiles Plenty's face was balanced across his saddletree.

"Where in blazes did them three come from?" said Nash, watching three Indians ride away in single file from Bull Hump's village. "From Smoke Rising's camp?"

Danford shook his head. The brim of his flat leather shako hat left most of his face in shadow. "Them ain't 'Rapaho. Them's Cheyennes."

"In a pig's ass! There's no Cheyenne camp hereabouts."

"Well, then, could be they just dropped down from the moon. But them's Cheyennes."

"Might be Cheyennes," said a third man in the group, which remained slightly down ridge from the other two. "But I scouted for the 2nd Cavalry, and I by God know shod horses when I hear them. Those red varmints're ridin' shod horses."

Danford nodded. "That they be, that they be. Makes a man a mite curious, don't it?"

Wes Munro had ordered Danford and his men to stand by during the assault by Cries Yia Eya and his renegades. Their orders were to sit tight unless the fight went badly for the rebels.

But *what* fight? Danford thought now. Those three upstart braves had quickly unstrung the attackers' nerves, and not one drop of Indian blood had stained the earth.

Danford realized it was pointless to attack the village now. His militia group was some two dozen strong, a formidable, well-armed force. But he knew the point was not simply to kill redskins—it was to make sure that the big chiefs were all drinking out of Munro's trough.

And those three Cheyennes, wherever the hell they'd come from, were obviously dead set against letting that happen. But how did they know about the plan for tonight? Munro had sworn it was secret.

He watched the three Cheyennes crest a long bluff, riding due east. The fat, butter-colored moon sat suspended on a low line of hills beyond them. For a moment the three figures slid across the lunar face, darkly silhouetted. It almost seemed as if they *had* fallen down out of the moon just in the nick of time, and were now returning inside.

White man's shod horses. They stole them then, thought Danford. That made them hostiles. But then, he agreed with the philosophy of some of the army commanders: *All* Indians were hostiles.

Wherever they came from, it was time to settle their hash. Danford had a job to do if he wanted to collect his wages. He told himself he damn straight wasn't about to let a trio of flea-bitten blanket asses come between *this* dog and his meat.

"Gee-up, you ornery, ugly, hard-cussin' bachelors of the saddle!" Danford called out to the rest. "Let's take some of the starch outta them red A-rabs!"

He put hard spur to his mount, and the big claybank leaped off down the side of the ridge. With a whoop, his men followed him.

As they returned to the river, the Cheyennes boasted as all Indian braves do after a victory.

"Brothers," said Little Horse, "did you see Cries Yia Eya's face as he flew over his pony's ears? I did not—all I could see was his rump!"

"And did you see the others flinch and duck when Little Horse rained buckshot down on them?" said Touch the Sky. "From their frightened faces, I thought we had perhaps woken the children!"

"Their bull was down," said Wolf Who Hunts Smiling, "so the herd ran over a cliff!"

All three Cheyennes laughed at that. For this moment, at least, the enmity between Wolf Who Hunts Smiling and the other two seemed forgotten.

But much had been left in doubt, and the three young bucks did not celebrate long as reality again set in. Cries Yia Eya had been taken prisoner even as they left, true. But how strong was his influence among the younger braves?

Exile from the tribe might not remove the threat. Unlike the Cheyenne, the Arapaho did practice capital punishment. But would Bull Hump, an old and ailing chief, be strong enough to enforce such a punishment?

Even worse, what lay ahead as the Tongue River wound its way into the country of the Shoshone, the Gros Ventres?

"Brothers," said Little Horse suddenly, "*why* ride back to the keelboat at all? True, we might be able to help as we did this night. But we already know the plans of the white dogs. Why not hurry back to our people, report this at council, and join the war party which will surely return?"

The other two reflected on this. It was Wolf Who Hunts Smiling who spoke.

"Because," he replied slowly, "it is better to stay and do the thing ourselves. The old hair-face spoke right. Kill the queen and the hive is lost. It will take many sleeps to return to camp, then ride out again painted for battle. *We* can kill these two whites and help our tribe avoid a terrible battle."

"But this decision would be without benefit of council. Chief Gray Thunder spoke wisely," objected Little Horse, "when he said no people are more terrible than the whites in their thirst for revenge when Indians kill their own."

"So? The war party you speak of would attract even more notice from the whites," said Wolf Who Hunts Smiling.

"True," agreed Touch the Sky. "But what if the two paleface dogs met a terrible accident? A death that could not be blamed on the red man? This is not unlikely on so hard and dangerous a journey."

Now the other two braves watched him closely, hungry for more.

"This time I think the hot-tempered Wolf Who Hunts Smiling is right," said Touch the Sky. "True, we have no permission from the Councillors to act on our own. But are we not warriors? Is our tribe, and many others, not in grave danger? These white devils have killed Smoke Rising. How many others would have gone under this very night? I say, we return to the boat and watch for our chance. These paleface swindlers drew first blood!"

Wolf Who Hunts Smiling stopped riding and thrust out his lance.

"I have ears for these words! This is not drawing first blood, so we are not sullying the Sacred Arrows. Let us swear on it, bucks! If we fall, it will be on our enemy's bones!"

All three warriors crossed lances and pledged themselves to the victory.

Yet despite this warrior's oath the three swore as one, Touch the Sky was worried. There was a strong, ambitious gleam in Wolf Who Hunts Smiling's eye—the same urgent glint he had seen on the night when, disobeying orders, Wolf Who Hunts Smiling had tried to raise a sleeping Pawnee's scalp. He had thus roused the enemy camp and caused the death of Swift Canoe's twin brother, True Son. To this

day Swift Canoe blamed Touch the Sky fo
that.

Wolf Who Hunts Smiling was young, with onl
17 winters behind him. But his ears were full o
tales of Indians with only 20 winters who ha
nonetheless led great tribes into battle. And Touc
the Sky now suspected that the good of the trib
had little to do with Wolf Who Hunts Smiling'
intentions—it was personal glory he wanted t
wrap himself in. No doubt he was determined t
have Munro's scalp dangling off his clout.

"Brothers!" said Little Horse, abruptly scatterin
Touch the Sky's thoughts. "Listen!"

They sat their ponies without moving, all thre
falling silent. Little Horse's keen ears were alread
legendary among the tribe. The trio was down
wind in a gentle breeze fragrant with the smel
of prairie flowers and sweet grass. The fa
moon shone big and yellow almost straigh
overhead.

Now Touch the Sky heard it—the stiff, lov
creaking of saddle leather, the jangle of cinche
and latigos and rowel-tipped spurs.

Caught up in their discussion, and still head
with thoughts of the tense encounter at Bu
Hump's camp, none of the braves had pai
attention to the long ridge on their right. Now
even as they stared in that direction, dozens o
well-armed riders charged over the ridge straigh
at them, gun muzzles spitting fire.

Touch the Sky realized immediately, as he du
his knees hard into the chestnut mare's flanks, tha
this must be Munro's militiamen.

"Ride like the wind itself, brothers!" shouted Lit
tle Horse. "Be one with your pony or sing the deat
song!"

Now lead whizzed past their ears with the sound of angry hornets. All three braves automatically dropped low and forward, into the defensive riding position for which their tribe was famous when bullets whined too close—hugging the pony's neck close, presenting a minimal target away from the direction of attack. All the whites might glimpse was a leg hooked over the pony's back, a face momentarily peering from under its neck.

"*Hiya!*" they urged their horses and rallied each other. "*Hiya hi-i-i-ya!*"

The attackers whooped and shouted curses behind them, their blood up for the kill. The ground thundered, horses nickered, more guns spoke their piece. Flying lead nipped at the braves' heels and tore up clumps of sod all around them.

Touch the Sky knew their only hope now was the strength and speed of their horses. These were all broncos, selected by Knobby as the best in the herd. Broncos could make fine and gentle horses. But Touch the Sky also knew that, despite the water-starving, beatings, blindfolds, and other tricks used by white men to break their spirit, now and then their former wildness came out. When that happened, broncos galloped with a reckless abandon that was dangerous for horse and rider.

Fortunately for the Cheyennes, the broncos' former wildness came out with a vengeance this night.

To the pursuing whites, the Cheyennes seemed to be simply an extension of the swift-as-lightning horses they rode with such astonishing skill. Steadily, one by one, the tamer mounts of the militiamen began to falter; the trio of wild Indians gradually opened the distance. Finally, when the

Cheyennes were swallowed up by a dense pine forest bordering the Tongue, Danford gave the command to cease the chase.

"Leave it alone for now, boys," he called out to his men. He holstered his big Navy Colt, butt forward to accommodate his left-handed cross-draw.

"The horses are played out. We'll ride closer to the river and make camp for the night. I got me a gut hunch we'll be seein' them bucks again real soon."

Chapter 12

But Fargo Danford didn't realize exactly *how* soon he'd be seeing the Cheyennes again.

As it turned out, he and his men made their camp less than a mile from the three braves' camp near the *Sioux Princess*. Danford picked this spot on purpose because he was due to report to his boss at the crack of dawn.

While his men snored in their bedrolls, Danford boiled himself a can of coffee. Then, with pockets of white mist still shrouding the river, he untethered the claybank and rode downstream to meet Wes Munro.

The three Cheyennes had already discussed this potential new danger of the militia reporting last night's chase to Munro. But they mistakenly believed the militia had crossed their trail by chance—they had no idea the hired outlaws had actually watched them ruin Cries Yia Eya's raid.

Very few whites, they all agreed, could distinguish tribes, especially in the dark. Chances were good the militia would have mistaken them for Dakota braves or neighboring Arapahos.

Thus lulling themselves with false security, exhausted, they slept soundly as Danford reported. He approached the boat quietly from upstream, and the Indian camp was well downstream from the keelboat. Thick mist separated their camp from the boat. The hissing chuckle of the current filtered out noises and made their sleep deeper. Danford had left his claybank in a spruce thicket before disappearing almost immediately inside the plank cabin.

"How'd things turn out last night?" Munro said in greeting. The keelboat skipper was still bare to the waist. A metal mirror was nailed to the wall. In the weak light of the coal-oil lamp, Munro was carefully shaving.

Hays Jackson sat at the deal table. His face was still sullen and lopsided with sleep, the left eye winking open and shut spasmodically. He poured whiskey into a metal cup of coffee and tossed it down in a few gulps.

"Jesus Christ in a buckboard!" said Danford, removing his shako hat and fanning it in front of his nose. He stared at Jackson. "Smells like something died and swole up bad in here."

"A bunch of goddamn wimmin worry about how they smell," said Jackson.

"Never mind that," said Munro impatiently. "Why do you two have to scrap like dogs?"

He concentrated closer in the mirror as he slid the straight razor over the bumps of his throat. "I asked you," he said to Danford, "how it turned out last night."

"It turned out flatter 'n a one-sided pancake," said Danford without further explanation.

Munro's hand stopped moving. His eyes shifted upward to find Danford's reflection in the mirror.

"Spell it out plain. I don't pay you top dollar to speak in riddles."

"Cries Yia Eya is trussed up tight in ropes, a prisoner of his tribe. And every damn one o' them weapons you give him is in the hands of braves loyal to Bull Hump. Is *that* plain enough?"

Red-mottled rage crept up from Munro's neck into his fresh-shaven face. He splashed water from the wash basin, rinsing off the remaining shaving soap. Only when the first, tight-templed throbs of anger passed did he speak again. His voice was dangerously low and calm.

"You mean to tell me you stood by and watched Bull Hump's braves whip Cries Yia Eya? And you and your men didn't pitch in?"

"Pitch in? Pitch in to *what*? Wes, I'm here to swear by the two balls of Christ there was no battle to pitch into! Thanks to three Cheyennes, it was all over faster than a starvin' man could swallow a chokecherry."

Danford was surprised. His remark about the Cheyennes nearly floored the other two men.

"Cheyennes?" repeated Munro in that same low, dangerously calm tone. "Three of them?"

Danford described the part the braves had played in defusing the raid.

"I tried to do for 'em," said Danford. "My word on it, we give 'em jip. But they had fresh, faster horses. White man's horses, though. They was all shod."

"Was one of the bucks," said Munro, "noticeably taller than the others? And the two smaller ones, was one stocky built, the other wiry and tough with slinking eyes that never stop moving?"

Danford's jaw went slack. "That they be, though I couldn't see no eyes. You know these Innuns?"

"Know them? Why, man, they've been drinking my coffee every day!"

Danford finally took his meaning. Understanding flashed in his eyes. "Say! You mean, them three jackleg boatmen you mentioned to me?"

His jaw clamped so hard the muscles were tightly bunched, Munro nodded. The same three boatmen who were coming between him and a wagon road that was only the beginning of huge profits and almost unlimited power.

Hays Jackson pushed away from the table, rising. He slid the Paterson Colt out of its holster. "The hell we waitin' on? Let's kill them slippery red niggers now."

"Put that iron away and sit down, you fool," said Munro. "You think you're just going to waltz up and kill *those* Indians? They might be young, but Gray Thunder knew what he was doing when he sent them. Don't sell a Cheyenne warrior short.

"Besides, I don't want them dead just yet. I need to know how much Gray Thunder knows. I need to know how he got wind of the scheme. And I damn sure need to know how much they've told to anyone else."

"See there? See there?" said Jackson. "I *told* you that red devil palavers English. Didn't I say he did?"

Munro ignored him, looking at Danford. "Did anybody see you come aboard?"

"Don't seem likely. I was quiet-like, and the mist is thick."

Munro glanced through the cabin doorway and

nodded with satisfaction. "It still is. Leave now. For all I know, they didn't even come back last night. But if they did they'll be coming aboard soon. I don't want them to see you."

"Should I have the boys resume the routine patrols?"

Munro shook his head. "No, not yet. Look here."

He stabbed an index finger into the navigation chart on the table. "There's a huge elbow bend in the river right before it reaches the fork with Frenchman's Creek. You know the spot?"

Danford nodded. "That I do. There's big salt licks there."

"That's the spot," said Munro. "Here's what I want you to do."

If Munro and Jackson harbored any new suspicions, Touch the Sky noticed no warning. Jackson was no more or less surly than usual when they reported on deck with the rest of the crew.

Munro, as always, spent most of his time over his charts and maps. Old Knobby greeted the trio with a stealthy wink and a reassuring nod. Then he turned quickly away again to tend to the horses and mules.

Nonetheless, as he glanced upriver through the clearing mist, Touch the Sky felt his still-developing shaman's sixth sense nettling him again.

Unfortunately, he had little time to ponder the feeling. He and Little Horse were both forced to keep a close watch on Wolf Who Hunts Smiling. Both braves had conferred in secret after yesterday's plan was formed. They agreed that the hotheaded, arrogantly proud youth would now seize the weakest excuse to kill Jackson and Munro.

They were determined not to let his blind quest for personal glory jeopardize the entire tribe.

If the *tribe* must be blamed, then *all* the Cheyenne warriors would tread the warpath first and earn the bloody punishment that would surely come. Otherwise, with luck and help from Maiyun, the Good Supernatural, the deaths of these two murdering land-grabbers would be "accidents" spawned by the dangerous river. The tribe had suffered enough from the white man's wrath.

All this tumbled like loose scree through Touch the Sky's head as he manned his pole to help shove the *Sioux Princess* away from the grassy bank. As usual the square sail lay flat and crumpled against the mast, as dead as a spent cartridge. When the boat reached midstream, the crew manned the oars. The river was wide hereabouts, fairly unencumbered for smooth rowing.

Something suddenly occurred to Touch the Sky: Despite Wolf Who Hunts Smiling's almost taunting stares and gestures, Jackson was just as deliberately ignoring him.

Why? He had never before shown such restraint. Why now? wondered Touch the Sky.

That feeling was back, a nagging little awareness like something half-remembered, half-forgotten. But once again he had no luxury to turn over and poke through his own thoughts. Now they were approaching a huge, sharp bend. The river suddenly constricted, boiling into white froth and making rowing impractical. Nor would poles ensure safe progress through all the boulders and other debris which naturally massed at river bends.

But smooth shelves of rock had been cut out by centuries of wind and current. They followed the bend around on both banks until the river wid-

ened again. The banks were easily wide enough
to accommodate many men.

"Man the cordelles!" shouted Jackson.

This was followed by the usual chorus of groans
from the Creole voyageurs. The two teams grabbed
the thick towing ropes and clambered over the
gunnels. Those waiting on deck fed the ropes overboard to their comrades as they swam ashore and
climbed up onto the rock ledges.

As the three Cheyennes prepared to leap out,
Touch the Sky again glanced upriver. Now the
sharp bend cut off most of his view.

Still, a cool feather of apprehension tickled the
bumps of his spine.

"Brothers!" he said suddenly to the other two.
"We are in danger! An enemy is hard upon us!"

Little Horse looked at him sharply. The sturdy
little brave was one of the few who had noticed
the mulberry-colored birthmark, shaped like an
arrowhead, buried past Touch the Sky's hairline.
This tall youth was also marked as a receiver of
visions. Arrow Keeper would never select any brave
to learn the shaman arts unless that brave already
possessed strong medicine.

"What do you mean?" demanded Little Horse.
"Quickly, brother! Speak words that fit in our
sashes!"

Touch the Sky shook his head, again staring
toward the bend. "I cannot. Yet just now I felt
it."

"You felt only your own fear," scoffed Wolf Who
Hunts Smiling. "Like women will do, you have
dwelled too long on the dangers we face. Now
the bowstring of your courage has frayed. Be a
man and do not fear any 'feeling.' That is a thing
of smoke."

"You goddamn red devils quit stalling!" shouted Jackson. "I said man that damn cordelle!"

"You are a pig's afterbirth!" Wolf Who Hunts Smiling said to him aloud in Cheyenne. "It is common knowledge that white men rut on sheep and turn the offspring into soldiers!"

Though Jackson couldn't understand these taunts, the other two quickly shut their companion up.

"Hump it!" Jackson snapped his whip on the deck. "Move your flea-bit asses!"

They leaped into the cold river, swam a few strokes, then waded ashore and pulled themselves up onto the nearest rock ledge. They took their usual place at the end of the line of men tugging the cordelle. Each man gripped the thick rope and strained. Little Horse was in front, followed by Wolf Who Hunts Smiling. Touch the Sky brought up the rear of the line.

"*Heave!*" shouted Jackson from the deck, establishing the cadence. "*Heave . . . heave . . . heave!*"

Soon sweat beaded up in his scalp and rolled down into his eyes. Sometimes Touch the Sky was bent almost double as he heaved forward against the rope. He tossed his head once to throw the sweaty, long locks back out of his eyes.

For a heartbeat, in the corner of his right eye, he saw the butt of the huge Navy Colt descending fast toward his skull. A moment later a color wheel exploded inside his head. His bones seemed to become all soft marrow as he collapsed on the ledge.

Chapter 13

Pain throbbed over his right temple, one moment dull, the next sharp. His entire body felt hot, and rivulets of sweat flowed down out of his thick hair, making it hard to open his eyes.

He opened them anyway, to nothing but the salt sting of sweat and a harsh yellow orb of relentless sun. Quickly he closed his eyes again. He tried to move his arms, his legs, but they refused to respond. Every slight movement of his head sent a fresh jolt of pain hammering into his skull.

"Thisen's comin' around," said an unfamiliar voice.

Touch the Sky cocked his head out of the sun and opened one eye. From this angle he saw the white canvas flap of the square sail, now billowing as a favoring wind finally filled it.

A boat, he remembered the keelboat. These hard

boards must be the planks of the deck beneath him, then. He still wasn't quite sure yet how he got there. But it felt like the boat was gliding along at a good clip. Why couldn't *he* move?

The sweat cleared from one eye. Now he saw Little Horse stretched out spread-eagle beside him on the deck. His wrists and ankles were bound in lengths of green rawhide. The rawhide had then been staked into the deck. Congealed blood traced the edges of a fresh wound on Little Horse's forehead. Flies had begun to land in the tacky mess.

He glanced to the other side and saw Wolf Who Hunts Smiling in the same plight, his jaw bruised and swollen, perhaps broken.

"Welcome to the white man's West," said Jackson's voice. A moment later the toe of a leather boot smashed into his ribs. Touch the Sky flinched as fresh pain wracked his body.

Now two faces peered down at him, harshly back-lit by the sun. Jackson's close-set eyes he recognized immediately, even without the nervous wink. The other man was a stranger. But no, he remembered that odd, flat hat—the leader of the exterminators of red men, who called themselves militia!

From the angle and warmth of the sun, Touch the Sky guessed it was late morning. Now the gates of memory had been flung wide, and he recalled being knocked cold on shore.

Jackson kicked him again harder, in the same spot. The force of the pain lifted Touch the Sky's strong back up inches off the deck, straining the green rawhide. But the strong thongs held.

"Thought you was a pretty crafty Injun, dintcha?" said Jackson. "Thought you was slicker 'n snot on a saddlehorn, hah? I wager this, blanket ass. Before that green rawhide shrinks all the way, you'll not only palaver in English, we'll have you singin' 'Loo-loo Girl!' "

Jackson kicked him in the face this time. The hob-nailed sole of his boot raked over Touch the Sky's cheek and split it open. Warm blood trickled into one eye.

Now Touch the Sky remembered why green rawhide had been used. It would shrink tight and firm in the sun, cutting off the blood and causing excruciating pain.

"Here's a lick for you too," said Jackson, kicking Little Horse in the groin. "Don't want to make you jealous of your pard."

The sickening thud of the kick made Touch the Sky wince. Another white man, the big baldhead one he had seen riding beside the militia leader last night, stood over Wolf Who Hunts Smiling.

"Thisen ain't quite woke up yet," said Heck Nash. "I hit him a mite hard. Maybe a little tonic water'll do the trick."

Moments later something warm splashed off the deck near him, and Touch the Sky realized with a shudder of disgust and murderous rage—the pale-face devil was making water in Wolf Who Hunts Smiling's face!

"H'ar now!" Touch the Sky recognized Old Knobby's angry voice. "Them's Injuns, mebbe, but a Christian man doan even treat a *dog* that low."

"You put a cork in it, you old pus-gut," said Jackson, "or we'll stretch your worthless, Injun-lovin' hide out beside 'em."

"Doan step in nothin' you can't wipe off," Knobby warned him defiantly. Now Touch the Sky could see him. The old man brandished his Kentucky over-and-under flintlock. "Ye'll speak direct to this gal afore ye hurt her sweetheart."

"You hear that old fart threaten me, Heck?" he said to the baldhead paleface. "I reckon old dogs growl even after they lose their teeth."

Wes Munro spoke quietly from the open doorway of the cabin, his words meant only for Jackson. "That old dog might yet kill both of us, you jack-ass. He had plenty of teeth when the Mandans and Crows hit us, didn't he? Don't force his hand. And you better chew on this too—the old man had to know the Indians have been riding the horses. Why do you suppose he's kept his mouth shut about it? Just whose colors do you think he's flying?"

"Sonofabitch," said Jackson. "Why, that old fart *has* got a set on him!"

Touch the Sky could hear only the sound of their voices, not the words. Munro added something else in his quiet voice. Then, mercifully, their tormentors left them alone for a while. But the sun and the shrinking rawhide quickly took over where the white devils had left off.

The pain in his wrists and ankles soon made his throbbing temple seem like a breeze caught in a tornado. He felt his hands and feet going numb as the thongs shrank in the hot sun. It felt like all four limbs were slowly being amputated.

Occasionally, Munro glanced out of the cabin at the three supine prisoners. He knew the Cheyenne tribe well enough to know that torturing a good brave for information was a tricky business, much like breaking green horses to leather. The spirit had to be broken first; the will to fight had to be destroyed.

That would be the job of those rawhide thongs,

plus a little extra hell thrown in for good measure now and then by Jackson and the militiamen. Hell, they had to have some fun. But Munro kept an eye on his men—he didn't want the Cheyennes beaten so senseless they couldn't answer his questions when the time came.

And they *would* answer his questions. All in good time. Plenty of investors back East had sunk capital into this venture. How could he return and report to them that savage, half-naked people who couldn't even record their own language had stumped him?

He had a plan. The threat of bodily harm to themselves might not be enough to break these stone-faced young warriors. But how would they respond if their refusal to cooperate hurt their companions instead?

Munro had studied the bucks closely during the voyage. The tall one who obviously knew English was tight as ticks with the powerfully built smaller brave. The other one, the sullen one with the furtive, swift-moving eyes, seemed aloof from both of them.

It was time to test his plan.

He went out on deck. The *Sioux Princess* still made good time, her square sail fat with favoring wind. A dozen men were rowing, assisting the wind against the current. Munro felt Etienne's gaze on him. But as usual when he glanced in the Creole leader's direction, the man was looking somewhere else.

That's another good reason, thought Munro, for cutting short the men's fun with the captives earlier. Though the voyageurs had remained aloof from the Cheyennes, a certain esprit bred from mutual suffering and hardship had sprung up. Etienne had watched Jackson with contemptuous hatred when he was kicking the braves, Munro recalled.

So it was best to keep it fast and quiet and effective.

Jackson and Heck Nash were sharing a bottle of whiskey at the stern of the boat. Munro waited impatiently until he had Jackson's attention. Then he nodded once. Jackson nodded back and handed the bottle back to Nash. On his way to join his boss, he paused to snatch a belaying pin out of its hole in the gunnel. It was a short but solid and heavy iron peg used for securing gear.

Touch the Sky was lost in a foggy delirium of pain. He was slow to register the image when Munro squatted down beside him and looked square into his face. His captor spoke in his halting but serviceable mixture of Cheyenne and Sioux.

"I know you speak English. For now, just tell me this. What orders did Gray Thunder give you?"

"Get downwind of me, you stinking mound of manure," said Wolf Who Hunts Smiling. He spoke with difficulty, the words slurred through his swollen jaw and lips. "Cheyenne braves will live to bull your mother and sisters while you watch!"

Munro ignored the snarling youth behind him. "I said, what orders did Gray Thunder give you?"

"He told me, as he told all of us, to work hard and not to shame our tribe."

"That's *all* he told you? You're sure?"

"He also said," Wolf Who Hunts Smiling interrupted, "that white men eat their newborns as will a cat! And that they smell worse than a camp dog's crotch! In these things he spoke straight."

"Cheyenne!" It was Little Horse who spoke, admonishing Wolf Who Hunts Smiling. "Are you a woman, to chatter so at our enemy? *Men* save their anger for deeds, not words."

"I'm saying it one last time: What else did your chief tell you?" repeated Munro.

"He reminded me to follow the Cheyenne way in all matters."

"Did he now? What else?"

"Nothing else. What have we done that is wrong?"

"What *you* just did wrong," said Munro, giving the signal to Jackson, "was that you refused to cooperate. And that refusal may have crippled your friend for life."

Pain jolted through Touch the Sky as Munro suddenly seized his head and turned it, forcing him to watch. Moving swiftly in spite of his bulk and drunkenness, Jackson pulled the belaying pin out from his sash. He bent low over Little Horse, took quick aim, then swung the pin with all his might, grunting loud at the effort. His blow smashed the tied-down warrior's right kneecap.

There was a fast, hard crack like green willow snapping. The surprised shriek this forced from Little Horse spooked the horses and made Nash drop his bottle overboard. Moaning, Little Horse went into shock and semiconsciousness.

Despite the terrible pain caused by the shrinking cords, Touch the Sky strained against them in rage. His murderous dark eyes shifted between Munro and Jackson. The latter chuckled as he rose again and slipped the iron peg back into his sash.

"Hell, it was like smashing a clamshell with a brick. *That* buck won't be doin' no war dances for a while."

Munro brought his smooth-shaven face within

inches of Touch the Sky's. "I'll be back later to ask you some more questions. Now you've seen what your refusal to help causes. Think about it. At least this time your friend is still alive."

Chapter 14

Touch the Sky did think about what Munro said. He thought long and deep, when the increasing pain from the shrinking rawhide would let him think.

He thought about it while Little Horse groaned at the double torture of shrinking cords and a shattered knee—this brave and true friend whose swift, sure movements had earned him his name. Never again would he glide with the lithe grace of a shadow.

Touch the Sky thought of this and much more. When Munro and Jackson returned, toward the end of the long afternoon, Touch the Sky had made up his mind. They were dead no matter what he said or didn't say. But saying one thing might get him untied. And that, at least, would be one last chance.

"How about it, friend?" Munro greeted him in

English. "You ready to talk terms?"

"I'm ready," he replied in the same language.

"Well, shit-oh-dear!" said Hays Jackson. "That belayin' pin must've inspired him."

"All right," said Munro. "Start by telling me what your chief knows."

"My chief," said Touch the Sky, "is Major Bruce Harding, Commanding Officer of the 7th Cavalry at Fort Bates."

Wolf Who Hunts Smiling had been about to hurl another insult in Cheyenne at the white dog. But he understood Touch the Sky's unexpected announcement. The words struck him with the force of fists. Now the rebellious Cheyenne buck fell silent, waiting for more.

Munro's face registered nothing at this. "What are you saying? Has your tribe signed a treaty with him? He's your treaty chief?"

"No. I'm saying he's my commanding officer. I was a forward observer with the Indian scouts assigned to his regiment. Now I'm on a longer mission to infiltrate the Cheyenne."

Jackson suddenly slapped his meaty thigh in amazement. "Hell 'n' furies! This is better 'n them shows where they got the two-headed cows! You believe the gall of this red nigger, sayin' he's a soldier?"

Munro was careful here. The claim did seem preposterous. On the other hand, this buck's English was spoken easily and with no accent. It was clearly the first language of his youth. And the War Department had indeed recently begun experimenting, infiltrating savage tribes with Indian spies loyal to the Stars and Stripes.

"If you're a spy," said Munro, "why did you speak up only after we hurt this brave?" He pointed at Little Horse.

"I'm not cooperating to protect the other two. I have nothing against them, they're good fighters and I share their blood. If I can help them, I will. I kept my mouth shut because that was my orders from Major Harding. But now I want to save my own bacon if I can. When you ordered that knee smashed, I knew then for sure you weren't just playing the larks."

Munro nodded. He was far from convinced, but it was a good, sensible answer.

He didn't know Major Harding personally, but he knew of him. Now Munro said, "What kind of man is your C.O.?"

Touch the Sky winced again at the tight-cutting pain of his rawhide bonds. He was aware that Wolf Who Hunts Smiling was listening to every word.

"A rulebook commander," said Touch the Sky, recalling what his friend Corey Robinson had told him. "A spit-and-polish man who can't tell a Sioux from a Cheyenne. He lets his junior officers make his decisions for him."

Munro said nothing. But this was exactly what he had heard about Harding.

"Who's your immediate superior?" said Munro. "The one you report to?"

"Lieutenant Seth Carlson."

In naming his enemy, Touch the Sky had taken a chance—Carlson had in fact been transferred far north of Ft. Bates as punishment for cooperating in Hiram Steele's attempt to run John Hanchon out of the mustang business. But if Munro knew this, he showed no sign of it.

"So what exactly *is* your mission for the Army?" said Munro.

This was the easiest part of his ruse. Touch the

Sky had grown up near a fort. Military formations, strategies, and thinking had been the stuff of everyday life.

"I communicate with forward observers by leaving messages in the forks of trees. I report anything that might be useful military intelligence. Exact numbers of braves, what kind of weapons and how many they're armed with, plans for major movements or raids. The Army already knows where most of the tribes pitch their summer camps. But by summer the horses are strong from the new grass, and the braves can fight on horseback naming their own terms. The Army wants to learn where the secret winter camps are located. Then they can attack when the snow and ice have the valleys locked. The ponies and the braves are weakest in winter."

"Hell, all that shines right to me," said Jackson. "I think this buck is tellin' the straight."

Wolf Who Hunts Smiling, ignored now, was ominously silent. He thought about everything he had just heard. What was Touch the Sky's motivation for saying these things? Everything he had just confessed to was an accusation hurled at him by members of the tribe. Had he cleverly made up a confession based on false accusations? Yet hearing him matter-of-factly state the words just now gave them a certain, bothersome ring of truth.

Could he be a spy after all? And even if he wasn't, could he not be claiming he was one to save himself from the fate awaiting the other two Cheyenne prisoners?

Munro too was wondering. This was a full-blooded Cheyenne. But if he was also an Army spy, he was a Cheyenne whose word would count for something with the military brass. True, he could prove true-blue soldier and ruin the wagon-road scheme—he certainly knew enough about it by now, if he chose to expose the plan.

But a man who had no qualms about selling out one race would just as quickly sell out another, if the price was right. And Munro could use such a man. His reports might be enough to bring in the soldiers against those tribes—like Bull Hump's—that refused to cooperate.

But Munro, unlike Jackson, was not yet convinced of the tall buck's story. Munro had survived on the frontier by taking nothing on faith and never trusting the next man. He left Touch the Sky and called Fargo Danford over.

"Where's your men?"

"Waitin' for me to meet 'em at Singing Woman Creek."

"We'll be there around nightfall," said Munro, gauging the remaining sun. "Listen, that new man you just put on the payroll . . ."

"Meeks? Sam Meeks?"

"That one. Didn't you say he was a snowbird? One who just deserted from the new regiment at Fort Bates?"

Danford nodded. "That new regiment formed special to hunt down Innuns. He slipped out after the first spring melt, said he was sick of eatin' beans and singin' 'Boots and Saddles.' "

Munro smiled at this news, adjusting one of his cuffs. He was the only man on board whose shirt was not fouled by dirt or sweat or blood. But a hard life spent following no law but his own had lent him a spur-trigger uncertainty it was not wise to challenge. Everyone who met him sensed it.

"Good. Tell him to come aboard when we reach the Singing Woman."

He returned to Touch the Sky's side and knelt down. "If you're telling the truth, we'll soon know," he told the Cheyenne prisoner. "And if you're telling the truth, I'll deal you in like a man and start by setting you free. The other two I can't do anything about, you have to understand—it's the same pressure a chief faces.

"Danford's men got their blood up chasing you three, but the kill never came. They want blood now. An Indian scout I can save. Not them. I'm not a strong enough chief. They've been drinking, and with women scarce, they're feeling mean and looking for a little fun. But you and I will talk some real terms, if your story proves out. You nail your colors to Wes Munro's mast, you'll come out of this a rich man."

Munro's eyes, two flat, hard chips of dark flint, held his.

"But if you're lying, buying time at my expense, all three of you die right there where you lay. Danford's men are upset. They've heard some story about Comanches dragging a white baby naked through cactus. Believe me, they plan on having some fun, and Cheyennes will do fine if Comanches aren't available."

Munro was watching him closely. Looking for the least sign, Touch the Sky knew, that all of this was a lie. That sign would also signal his death.

"That's fine by me," said Touch the Sky. "But these cords hurt like hell. You're all armed—can't you at least cut me loose while we're waiting?"

One chance, Touch the Sky thought. One wild chance was all he asked. One lunge for the knife in

Jackson's sheath. Knobby was no doubt watching everything. The old mountain man would get off at least two good shots, buying some time to cut the other two free. Wolf Who Hunts Smiling could fight, at least try to escape. But Little Horse could not even move.

Still, he could hold a weapon! What was the alternative to such wild schemes? Only slow, sure, agonizing, and humiliating death. Better to die like Cheyennes, uttering war cries with their last living breath. One chance was all he asked.

Munro considered the request for some time, watching the Cheyenne's face closely. Whatever he read there, his response showed that he did know Indians.

"No. We'll wait until Sam has a good look at you."

The green rawhide not only constricted around his limbs, it also drew tighter and tighter at the stakes until Touch the Sky was arched like a warrior's bow, forced to bend his back to relieve the pressure.

This same pressure bent the others too, causing incredible contortions of pain to Little Horse's ruined right knee. Now he had regained awareness and bore his pain in a numb silence.

Sunlight bled slowly from the sky, and the air took on the first evening chill. Touch the Sky knew, from the detail of voyageurs ordered to the poles, when they had reached the juncture with Singing Woman Creek. The sail had already been lowered. The first frogs of evening were beginning to sing when the *Sioux Princess* tacked close to shore and threw down her boarding plank.

Touch the Sky guessed, from the amount of whooping and cheering and shouting at the near-by camp, that the drinking had begun early. The planks trembled under him as more men in heavy boots boarded, clumping their way heavily toward the bound Cheyennes.

"That's what I'm sayin', Mr. Munro," said the voice he guessed was Sam Meeks. "Fort Bates ain't never used but Pawnees for scouts. And this Seth Carlson, he got orders out just after I joined up. He had a set-to with a big tall Cheyenne buck, and he lost."

Moments later the harsh smell of liquor assault-ed his nose. Daylight was fading fast now, and several coal-oil lamps were already lit. Somebody thrust one close to his face.

"And right there's the buck who whipped him!" said Meeks triumphantly. "Spy? My sweet aunt! This here's the slippery hoss that sent Carlson somersaultin' 'cross the plains! Hell, half the 7th Regiment was poking steel after this one and his pard here with the swole-up knee. Can't say I've ever seen the other one, though, and I'm one tends to mark down an Indian's face for later."

For a moment Munro looked as if he'd just swal-lowed something that didn't agree with him. But it passed, and his face took on its usual calm wari-ness. He slipped one of the dueling pistols out of his sash and fired it into the air.

The flat report startled everyone into silence.

"You men on shore!" he called out. "Tonight it's good liquor and it's compliments of the Over-land Company! Come aboard and broach a keg in friendship!"

A rousing cheer greeted this and men began hurrying onto the boarding ramp.

"There's also entertainment tonight!" shouted Munro. "We've captured three Cheyenne savages that tried to slit our throats while we slept!"

This brought another cheer and a few shouted oaths. The current Apache and Comanche uprisings to the south had paralyzed Texas and the Arizona Territory and spread fear far north. Now all was pandemonium as more of the hardcase militiamen joined the knot boarding.

It was one of Danford's men, having crossed to the pen to admire some of the horseflesh, who first saw it—the rapid sweep of flames just now engulfing the stern!

"Sweet Jesus Christ!" he said to himself. Then, almost as an afterthought, he yelled as loud as he could, "Fire!"

Chapter 15

Lying trapped on the deck, Touch the Sky felt the mood change from hostility to panic.

"Fire!" someone shouted again. The deck shook and vibrated under him as the men rushed toward the stern. The same stiff breeze that had filled the square sail all afternoon now wafted the first billowing clouds of harsh smoke to Touch the Sky's nostrils.

The boat pitched wildly at anchor as the horses panicked, rearing up, leaping up out of the shallow pen and forcing men to jump overboard to get out of their way.

"What's on the spit, tadpole?" a familiar voice suddenly said in his ear.

"Knobby!"

"Boy, you better hump it like a hound with his ass afire," said the old-timer grimly as he sliced his Bowie through the rawhide thongs binding Touch the Sky. "That-air blaze I set ain't gonna burn forever."

Knobby leaped across to free Wolf Who Hunts Smiling as Touch the Sky, body protesting in pain, sat up and quickly rubbed some life back into his dead, swollen limbs. Knobby must have ducked into the cabin first: Their weapons lay piled on the deck nearby.

"Shove that cut rawhide in your legging sash," said Knobby. "No need the others findin' it quick and knowin' how you was sprung."

"What about Little Horse?"

"Doan be a bigger fool 'n God made you, sprout! Lookit! Twixt that-air smashed knee and that bash he took on the brain-pan, he ain't goin' nowheres. You two jist rabbit for help or all three of ye're as good as planted!"

Old Knobby was right and Touch the Sky knew it. The old man had just risked his life for them, and he still had a lot to explain to Munro. Either they insisted on taking Little Horse, and died now trying to get him ashore, or they ran hard and lived to fight another day, perhaps saving Little Horse. It wasn't much of a choice, nor was there time to debate—already the flames were under control. Any second now someone would glance forward and see them.

Wolf Who Hunts Smiling too stumbled a few times trying to take a first step on his numb limbs.

"This hoss is dust," said Knobby, heading back toward the hubbub at the rear. "Keep your powder dry, lads!"

In a moment he had disappeared in the confusion. Touch the Sky was casting a last, regretful glance at Little Horse when Wolf Who Hunts Smiling urged in his ear, "Into the river, buck, and cry for your friend later!"

They leaped off the prow, stiff muscles screaming in pain, and sliced into the cool river water. Behind them, horses still nickered in fright and greasy black smoke clouds still darkened the twilight sky. No one had seen them leap. They decided to strike for the opposite, more heavily wooded bank.

They had not quite reached the middle of the river when Hays Jackson's voice roared, "What in tarnal hell? The Innuns're loose!"

"There!" someone else shouted. "There, in the river, see 'em?"

"Put at 'em, boys!" yelled Fargo Danford. "It's like shootin' fish in a barrel!"

The sun was down, but there was still plenty of light for aiming. A terrific volley of rifle and pistol fire churned the water into foam all around the two fleeing Cheyennes. Touch the Sky took a quick breath and swam deep, his chest scraping river bottom. The deadly hail of lead followed him down, making hollow pinging noises underwater.

He lost track of Wolf Who Hunts Smiling. His lungs were soon bursting for air, but Touch the Sky refused to surface again until he struck the opposite bank. His head emerged at the same moment as his comrade's. They scuttled up out of the water like wading birds fleeing from a snake, bullets still humming past their ears and zwipping through the tall bunchgrass.

There was a savage explosion from the starboard gunnel as someone fired a blunderbuss. The eight-ounce ball whistled between Touch the Sky's legs and ploughed into the bank, kicking up a geyser of dirt and grass. Another blunderbuss fired, and a sapling just beside Wolf Who Hunts Smiling snapped in two.

Bullets nipping at their heels, they finally reached the protection of the trees. But now they could hear the sounds of pursuit as their white enemies, mounted on horseback, began fording the Tongue.

Anyone watching the two youths move would have thought they were old men tied up with stiff joints. Feeling had still not returned to Touch the Sky's swollen feet, and Hays Jackson's brutal kicks had left his rib cage a mass of tender bruises. Each deep breath felt like a spike being stomped into him.

But the sounds of deadly pursuit, not far behind them, turned those clumsy feet into wings. Unencumbered by horses, they were able to penetrate the thickets and brambles that riders would have to bypass. By the time darkness had finally settled in, the sounds of the chase had given way to the usual nocturnal chorus of the forest.

"I am for traveling through the night," said Touch the Sky. "It is all downriver to our camp. We follow the Tongue to Bear Creek, then to the Powder."

"I have ears for this," said Wolf Who Hunts Smiling. "We can hollow out a canoe from one of these soft logs. We must return to camp, alert the council, then join the war party which must intercept the keelboat and destroy those white devils."

"And save Little Horse and Knobby," added Touch the Sky.

"Little Horse will be dead," said Wolf Who Hunts Smiling flatly. "Nor do I think the old hair-face will still be above the ground. The whites will soon guess that he helped us."

"This one has helped you more than once," said

Touch the Sky, "yet you say you hate all whites."

"He is a warrior to be respected. He knows even more than my cousin Black Elk about the warrior arts. But never forget that for all we have seen the hair-face do, there is even more we did not see. He has scalped red men in his youth—I have seen the scar on his head, his cold eye and steady hand when the battle is on! *You* have seen trouble, but never have you been forced as I have to watch while Bluecoats cut your father down like cattle, laughing and congratulating themselves and paying off bets on the kill!"

For once Wolf Who Hunts Smiling had not spoken merely to taunt him. But almost as if sensing he had shown too much feeling, the younger brave now spoke in his usual, arrogant tone. It was another reminder of the battle looming between them, a reminder that their two ambitions took vastly different forms.

"Put your friends out of your mind. This leaves more room to nurture vengeance after we return. Those stinking dogs lifted their legs and made water on me! I will lead the young warriors in their first combat. We shall kill so many that Arrow Keeper will have to declare a Scalp Dance to give thanks! Little Horse and the brave old hairy-faced one shall be avenged many times over."

Still, as the two Cheyennes began desperately whittling the center out of a cottonwood log to make a hasty dugout, Touch the Sky clung to hope for his two friends.

"Alert the bands all up and down the river," said Wes Munro. "Watch the land routes and post sentries along the water. And make the order clear: Shoot to kill. These are dangerous braves."

Fargo Danford merely nodded, too disgusted to muster the usual false congeniality toward his employer. He had promised his boys a big she-bang tonight, and now Munro was closing down the show.

"I'll put the word out," he said. "But say, who can blame 'em if they ain't too keen for it? They was promised top-shelf liquor. Now they're sent off without any."

Munro was quiet after this, staring out across the dark silence of the river. He, Hays Jackson, and Fargo Danford stood just outside the cabin of the *Sioux Princess*. Most of the men had gone ashore to their old camp, sent by Munro in his rage after the escape.

Now he had cooled off enough to know it was dangerous to push it with these men.

"You're right," he told Danford. "They can take the liquor with them. Just leave me in peace on the boat."

"Say! That's mighty white of you, Wes. I'll see to it personal that them two Cheyenne whelps get kilt. What about the one that's left?"

"Leave him. He's unconscious now anyway. He might draw the other ones back. Just make sure you alert the rest of the bands. I want that Powder River camp watched. The first sign of a war party forming, all the militia will rendezvous at the boat."

"Got 'er," said Danford.

Danford's boot heels were still drumming on the boarding ramp when Munro turned to Jackson.

"How do you figure that fire got set?"

Jackson's face was a blur in the darkness, but Munro could smell him plain enough. He stepped carefully upwind of his lackey.

"One of the horses kicked over a coal-oil lamp, mebbe?"

"Maybe. But where was the old man when the fire broke out?" said Munro. "I saw him later, returning from this direction."

"I catch your drift," said Jackson. "The old fart lit it hisself, then cut the bucks loose."

"That's what I'd wager," said Munro.

"Pus-gut old sonofabitch."

Both men stood in the slanted shadow cast by the cabin, watching Knobby measure out grain for tomorrow's feed.

"He's been in this right from the jump," said Munro with sudden conviction. "He knew the tall buck from before. He must have sneaked ashore during that ceremony, met with him. It's been that old codger all along."

"Like he told us, he's got his rifle to hand. He's expectin' us."

Munro nodded. "But he'll drink himself to sleep like he always does. Just be patient."

Old Knobby did get drunk, as usual. But he also took extra precautions when he fell asleep.

Instead of his usual bedroll on deck, he made a crude shakedown bed right in the middle of the pen amongst the horses. He knew from long years of experience that horses would avoid stepping on humans. Curled up around his Kentucky over-and-under, he drifted off to sleep hidden behind a score of milling horses.

Sometime late in the night, one of the horses nickered. The old mountain man sat up, instantly wide awake.

There was a loud, menacing click as he cocked the hammers. The river was silent except for the low hum of insects, the gentle lapping of the water against the hull. A clear night sky had been dotted wide with blazing stars.

"Come on, then," he said softly into the horse-fragrant darkness around him. "Ol' Patsy Plumb here has got a kiss fir ye."

Another horse nickered, several moved nervously. Knobby kept his head down below their bellies, watching for legs wearing pants.

Suddenly he heard a soft plop as something was thrown in among the animals. There was a slither of movement in the corner of his eye, an abrupt stirring among the horses. Then Knobby saw, in a stray patch of moonlight on the deck, that it was a fat brown river snake that had been tossed into the pen.

The snake panicked at all the dangerous hooves. The horses were equally panicked by the sudden presence of a reptile. They reared back all around it, leaving Knobby exposed in his crude pallet.

A light suddenly flared inside the cabin, and Knobby swung his rifle in that direction, distracted.

That was when Jackson stepped up behind him and slugged him hard on the side of the head with the belaying pin.

The flintlock clattered to the deck. Knobby gave one surprised grunt before he sprawled over on top of it.

Jackson kicked him several times for good measure.

"Drag him up here," said Wes Munro quietly from the cabin. "Stake him out next to the Indian. A man likes to be surrounded by his friends when he's dying."

Chapter 16

Touch the Sky and Wolf Who Hunts Smiling quickly discovered that death now lurked at every turn in the river, behind every deadfall.

They finished hollowing out their dugout while the Grandmother Star still blazed brightly in the north. They lugged the canoe down to the river and slipped into the quick-moving current. For the rest of that night they made good time. Only an occasional embarrass or beaver dam slowed them down.

By sunrise they were exhausted and hungry. They stashed the dugout in a thicket and killed a pair of rabbits. Spitting them on the same arrows that killed them, they risked a small fire and roasted them. After feasting on tender rabbit meat and cold river water, they forced themselves to move well downriver from that spot in case their smoke had been spotted. Then they crawled into

a cedar copse and slept until the sun's warmth
signaled mid-morning.

Almost immediately after they took to the river
again, they encountered danger.

The Tongue had narrowed as it passed through
a rock canyon. The banks rose steep and craggy
on both sides, slippery, deep-seamed rock carved
out through countless eons. They steered the canoe
with crude paddles they had fashioned out of
squares of bark lashed tight to willow branches.
Several boulders, made dangerous by the speed of
the current, lay just beneath the frothing surface of
the river. These hidden dangers required all their
concentration.

Neither of them saw the telltale glint high overhead as sunlight caught the brass butt plate of a
Sharps percussion carbine. Word of their escape
was rapidly being relayed downriver. Marksmen
were being positioned at key points.

The churning of the river was deafening in this
constricted, rock-lined gorge. The two Cheyennes
never heard the report of the carbine.

A narrow water spout shot up just in front of
Touch the Sky's paddle. Another. His curiosity was
deepening into a sense of danger when a bullet
thwacked into the front of their dugout, chipping
bark into his eyes.

"Jump!" shouted Touch the Sky.

He flew out one side of the dugout, Wolf Who
Hunts Smiling the other, just as the next shot
embedded itself where Touch the Sky had been
sitting.

They were forced to trust their weapons to the
dugout. Once again the two Cheyennes swam deep,
surfacing only when their lungs ached hard for air.
They continued swimming deep until they reached

a flat, peaceful stretch of forest well past the small canyon.

"Look!" Touch the Sky pointed.

The dugout had become wedged between two boulders. Several bullets were embedded in it. But none had penetrated under the waterline. Their rifles would have to be dried off some, but were still safely stowed along with their bows and fox-skin quivers filled with arrows.

"Buck," said Wolf Who Hunts Smiling, "we are alive only because Maiyun chose to smile on us. We must be more vigilant. Word of our escape precedes us by land."

Touch the Sky nodded. Again the rigorous warri-or training first taught to them by Black Elk came into crucial play. By day and by night the two Cheyennes moved swiftly, silently, stopping only during the day to snatch a few hours' rest. Often they took turns fitfully napping in the dugout

They looked like the walking wounded after a terrible and long battle campaign. Deep pouches of exhaustion formed under their eyes. Wolf Who Hunts Smiling's jaw was still bruised and swollen, as were Touch the Sky's ribs. Raw scars circled their wrists and ankles like bloody bracelets, the legacy of the rawhide thongs.

Despite their exhaustion, they remained ever alert for the warnings of frightened shore birds and the angry scolding which jays reserved for intruders. Their new vigilance was rewarded: Twice they were able to spot hidden marksmen before they themselves were sighted.

They eluded the first one, hidden in a deadfall where Bear Creek joined the Tongue, by lugging their dugout ashore and laboriously carrying it around his position. But this was time-consuming, exhausting work, especially in their present condition.

"The next one we see," vowed Wolf Who Hunts Smiling, "will taste the edge of my knife! At this pace we will be in the cold moons before we reach our village."

"We cannot kill all of them," said Touch the Sky. "Nor outwit so many. Travel on the river is too dangerous and slow. We need horses."

"As long as you are wishing," said Wolf Who Hunts Smiling, mocking him, "why not wish for wings so we might simply *fly* back? Just how do you plan to get these horses? With shamanism?"

"There are ways without magic," said Touch the Sky. His constant worries about Little Horse and Knobby made him desperate to cover more ground more quickly. "You are too quick to rush in fighting, when using your brain would be better."

"And you," said Wolf Who Hunts Smiling, "are too quick to make clever plans like a woman when a warrior's rash courage is the best plan."

"When it is time to close for the kill," said Touch the Sky, "I think of nothing but finding my enemy's warm vitals. But until that time forces itself, I put the welfare of my tribe before personal glory."

"So you say now. This is not what you told the white pig Munro when you begged him to loosen your bonds. *Then* you were ready to play the turncoat Ute for him!"

Anger sent hot blood into Touch the Sky's face. He had been lying to buy time, and Wolf Who Hunts Smiling had to know that. But now their dugout was nearing a wide bend and Touch the Sky bit back his retort. The militiamen liked to wait at such places. It was time to leave words behind and rely on his senses.

They had just entered the bend when a flock of startled sandpipers rose from the shore ahead of them, from a point out of sight just past the bend.

Both Cheyennes saw the birds at the same moment. Tired muscles screaming at the strain, they quickly back-paddled against the current and angled toward the bank. They hid their dugout behind some hawthorn bushes. Then, sticking to the thickets and willow rushes, they crept forward with their rifles held close to their chests.

When they were almost through the bend, they spotted them.

About a half-dozen well-armed whites sat their horses, sharing a smoke break with another man on the ground.

"The hair-face militiamen," whispered Wolf Who Hunts Smiling, "checking with one of their sentries."

Touch the Sky nodded. "Your knife will not silence all these."

"No," Wolf Who Hunts Smiling said grimly. "Now we lose more precious time carrying the dugout."

"Not this time," said Touch the Sky, thinking again of Little Horse and Knobby. Both men had saved his life, had fought beside him in pitched battles and proven themselves brave warriors. If there was a chance that either of them was still alive, that chance got slimmer with every hour wasted.

"On horseback," said Touch the Sky, "we can reach our tribe in one sleep. This is where we trade our dugout for horses. Hear my words."

His plan was simple and reckless, and thus it appealed to Wolf Who Hunts Smiling. They worked quickly, before the riders could leave. First the younger brave returned to the dugout for the rest of their weapons. Then, leaving his rifle with Wolf Who Hunts Smiling so he could move unencumbered, Touch the Sky worked his way into the thick brambles and bushes beside the river.

He waited until Wolf Who Hunts Smiling had sneaked into position behind a huge elm tree near the white men.

Then, quite boldly, he stepped into the open as if unaware the others were present.

"Look yonder!" shouted one of the militiamen.

The growth hereabouts was too dense to chase a man on horseback. As Touch the Sky leaped back behind cover, his heart thumping hard against his ribs, the first bullets sliced through the brush all around him. He made plenty of noise as he ran, hoping the whites would give chase on foot.

They did, though he couldn't be sure how many. Their clumsy, heavy boots made it ridiculously easy to track their progress as he led them on a wild run away from the river. Occasionally, when they seemed to be slowing, he showed just enough of himself just long enough, teasing them into another shot and more clumsy pursuit. But now and then a bullet whanged past his ears, dangerously close, and reminded Touch the Sky this was no child's game.

Then a single rifle report back near the river made Touch the Sky's blood surge with hope—and sent the whites back to the bend in a near panic.

Touch the Sky made his way quickly downriver to the copse where he had arranged to meet Wolf Who Hunts Smiling. The younger brave waited impatiently for him. His face was triumphant and arrogant as he handed the reins of a powerfully built bay to Touch the Sky. He also led a spotted gray mare whose chest was thickly ridged with muscles. Both animals had clearly been selected for endurance.

"As you said, they left only the one paleface to watch their mounts," he said. "And though I had no time to raise his hair, another white enemy has crossed over!"

The horses were saddled, which caused Wolf Who Hunts Smiling considerable trouble and scowling at first. But soon they were making good time as they crossed the open tableland between the Tongue and the Powder, every heartbeat bringing them deeper into Cheyenne country and closer to their people.

"Wolf Who Hunts Smiling and Touch the Sky approach camp!" shouted the crier, racing his pony up and down the clan circles. "They ride in on white man's horses!"

It was early morning, the mist still floating like pale smoke over the Powder River. Curious Cheyennes spilled forth from their tipis, congregating in the central clearing before the council lodge. Honey Eater was among them, her lower lip caught between her strong white teeth in her nervousness. She felt Black Elk's angry, jealous eyes watching her every moment. She tried to keep the deep concern and relief from showing in her face.

But when she finally spotted Touch the Sky, her breath snagged in her throat.

The blood-encrusted gash over his temple, bloody and raw bracelets around ankle and wrist, the huge, grape-colored bruises on his ribs, the arrow wound in his thigh—these spoke eloquently of such suffering that tears of pity formed on her eyelids.

Then, as the two warriors rode up, Touch the Sky's eyes found hers.

The hunted-animal hardness left his troubled gaze. The suggestion of a smile replaced the grim, determined slit formed by his lips. Her fragile beauty again took his breath away and made the blood throb in his temples. And he told himself again, *this is why I fight*.

But Black Elk was watching both of them, and the light smoldering in his eyes was clearly not a welcoming fire as was hers.

"Father!" said Wolf Who Hunts Smiling, spotting Chief Gray Thunder as he swung clumsily down from the saddle. "Have ears for my plea and call the Councillors together *now*!"

Gray Thunder silently studied his two bruised and bloodied young warriors.

"You left on the white man's boat," he said at last, "and now you return on stolen ponies, bearing the marks of much suffering and pain. This is how the white men used you, Cheyennes, in spite of their word that you would be respected. Yes, the Councillors will meet as is the way. I would hear your tales. But the greater part of them is told in these scars and hurts you bear. Soon the Arrows will be renewed for battle!"

Now Gray Thunder nodded at the camp crier, who was soon covering the well-packed paths of camp as he summoned the Council of Forty to the meeting lodge. The sense of urgency was strong, and the usual ceremonies of prayer and smoking to the directions were suspended.

Gray Thunder called on both braves to speak. Touch the Sky reported in detail everything he had overheard about the scheme to build a wagon road through the heart of Plains Indian homelands. Wolf Who Hunts Smiling admitted he understood less of the English, but verified these things.

Gray Thunder showed little emotion, though he nodded with approval at Wolf Who Hunts Smiling's description of the aborted coup by Cries Yia Eya, and his subsequent capture by the Dakota people.

"There is nothing else for it now but a battle!" said Touch the Sky when his companion had finished. "Chief Smoke Rising has been murdered. More villages will be divided, more of the 'private treaties' signed. If Munro is allowed to complete this journey, his talking papers will speak against us, and they will speak a death sentence! Soon all red men will lose the lush grass and the buffalo. They will be confined to the arid, empty lands where the Apaches hide."

These words stirred several headmen to voice agreement. Touch the Sky had only spoken from his heart. But when he finished, he saw Arrow Keeper eyeing his apprentice with pride and admiration. A red man who could speak well at council would go far indeed!

"The stones will speak," said Gray Thunder. "These whites have killed not only Smoke Rising, but Smiles Plenty and his fellow hunters. For these crimes and others, I too counsel for war against these whites. Our fight is not with the hired boatmen. Those who do not fire at us will not be fired upon. But the dogs named Munro and Jackson must die with their murdering 'militia.'"

"My warriors are ready," said Black Elk. "I was for greasing their bones with war paint from the first moment I heard his honeyed tongue spreading its lies!"

Black Elk and Touch the Sky had carefully avoided meeting each other's eye. Both were well aware there was an unsettled score between them. And Black Elk had noticed the approval Touch the Sky's words inspired from some elders. But rumors about Black Elk's jealousy had spread through camp, and he knew it would not be wise to speak against his enemy. So now he passed a quick signal to Swift Canoe, who was eager to snipe at his enemy at every opportunity.

Swift Canoe spoke: "Fathers and brothers! It has not been so long since River of Winds, one of our most trusted warriors and hunters, reported that Touch the Sky is a spy for the Long Knives! I saw with my own eyes when he met with a Bluecoat chief, when he left messages for this chief in the forks of trees! Is it wise to rush into battle against whites now at *his* bidding?"

"Wolf Who Hunts Smiling is your friend," said Touch the Sky. "He has been with me for this entire voyage, and he too counsels for war."

A long silence followed this comment. All of the Councillors looked at Wolf Who Hunts Smiling, waiting.

"Yes, I counsel for war," he said. "But as for Touch the Sky's loyalties, I say Swift Canoe is wise to advise caution."

Now Wolf Who Hunts Smiling looked only at Gray Thunder. "Touch the Sky begged that white jackal Munro to loosen his bonds. He boasted how he was a spy for the hair-faced soldiers. He boasted how cleverly and easily he spoke out of both sides of his mouth. He compared himself to those Indians who raise one hand in greeting while with the other they kill you!"

Wolf Who Hunts Smiling had not missed the increased tension between Black Elk and Touch the Sky. Now Wolf Who Hunts Smiling met his older cousin's eye and held it as he added, "He also boasted openly of the joys of tasting the fruits of both race's women, without owing responsibility to either."

The furrow between Gray Thunder's eyes grew ominously deeper as he stared at Touch the Sky. "Are these charges true?"

The youth felt his face flush. These last words were an outright lie, but the first part had been true enough. "I spoke some words like these, Father. But they were bent words. I wanted the white dog to untie me."

"I was in pain too," said Wolf Who Hunts Smiling. "So was Little Horse. *We* did not forsake our tribe just to be untied and made more comfortable."

Touch the Sky rose in anger from his spot beside the center lodge pole. "You know full well that I did not seek 'comfort.' I only wanted the chance to free you and Little Horse and go for my enemy."

Though he held his face impassive, inwardly Wolf Who Hunts Smiling was gloating. Here stood his worst enemy in the tribe, showing his embarrassed anger in his face like a white man! Of course the wily Cheyenne buck knew Touch the Sky hadn't intended to cooperate with the whites. But it was dangerous to let this tall newcomer win too much influence among the elders. Again Wolf Who Hunts Smiling had managed to sew seeds of doubt amongst Gray Thunder and the Council of Forty.

"This incessant bickering only turns over old dirt," said Gray Thunder, "without bearing fruit. Our purpose now is to vote with our stones. Do the Cheyenne people ride the warpath against this land-stealing murderer?"

Half of the Council of Forty were voting Headmen. A pouch containing 40 stones—20 white moonstones and 20 black agates—was passed among them. Each voting Councillor removed a stone of his choice and kept it hidden in his palm. When the pouch returned to Gray Thunder, he shook it out on the robes in front of him: 20 white moonstones formed a pile.

Gray Thunder stared at the unanimous yes vote. Then he gazed around at the Headmen and addressed them as one:

"The red man did not send out the first soldier, we only sent out the second. Now the tribe has spoken with one voice. The Shaiyena people are at war!"

Chapter 17

No time was wasted after Gray Thunder's announcement.

Cheyenne warriors seldom mounted an offensive battle without painting and dressing and making their offerings to the sacred Medicine Arrows. Warriors often chose to run away, with no loss of honor, rather than fight before they had thus acquired strong medicine. So it was announced that the Renewal of the Arrows would take place that same day. The war party would then ride out well before the sun went to her resting place.

Cheyenne and Sioux scouts had already reported on the militiamen, and the warriors knew these well-armed hair-faces would likely join the battle as mercenaries for Munro. However, no one knew their actual numbers. But between the militia and the big-thundering guns of the *Sioux Princess*, a hard, bloody fight was expected.

In the past Touch the Sky had made offerings
to the Medicine Arrows before riding into battle.
But today, for the first time, he would assist Arrow
Keeper in conducting the ceremony.

Always at the back of his mind was his concern for Little Horse and Old Knobby. Though
he knew that escaping had been the only chance
for *all* of them, he still felt gnawing doubts—despite
Little Horse's crushed knee and the lack of time,
could he have freed him? But how? And Knobby—
Munro and Jackson would not be slow to guess
who must have cut the Cheyennes loose. The old
man had known that when he did it, sacrificing his
life to give them a slim hope of escape.

This constant worrying about his friends alter-
nated with rage toward Wolf Who Hunts Smiling.
The wily brave's clever posturing at the council
had once again revived the specter of Touch the
Sky's supposed treachery. How much longer, he
wondered bitterly, must he be punished for the
crime of having been raised by whites?

All these thoughts and worries scurried through
his head like frenzied insects as he dressed and
painted for the Renewal. He had just donned the
mountain-lion skin Arrow Keeper had given him
when he heard his name called harshly outside of
his tipi.

No mistaking that deep, sullen bark: Black Elk.

Touch the Sky threw aside the entrance flap.

"Your war leader would speak with you," said
Black Elk's haughty voice.

The young warrior was resplendent in his battle
finery of war bonnet, bone breastplate, and leggings reinforced with stiff collars of leather to protect from lance points and tomahawks. His coup
stick was heavy with tufts from enemy scalps, died

bright red and yellow. Black Elk's face was streaked red and black for battle. Again Touch the Sky felt a slight shiver move up his spine as he looked at the dead-leather flap of severed ear sewn back on to Black Elk's skull with buckskin thread.

"Then speak," said Touch the Sky curtly. He was in no mood to conciliate his enemies within the tribe. He had learned that conciliation was seen as weakness.

"I am your war chief! You will not use this tone with me."

"And *I* am a warrior who has counted coup and slain enemies in battle. I have killed whites, Pawnees, and Crows in defense of my tribe. The council has honored me for my bravery. You will not talk down to me as if I were a dog. This is my tipi. Speak your words and then leave."

"As you wish, *shaman*. I am here to say only this. You have used your black arts to beguile Honey Eater. You have cast some sort of spell over her and hold her enthralled. But she is *my* bride! Her clan accepted my gift of horses and vows have been exchanged.

"So know this, if I ever see you exchange even one word with her, I swear by this coup stick to finish what our chief's summons interrupted. My blade will open you from throat to rump and spill out your guts for the maggots!"

His threat still hung in the air like bitter smoke long after Black Elk had turned and left. Touch the Sky finished dressing and painting. Then he met Arrow Keeper in the clearing before the council lodge. The four sacred arrows in their coyote-fur pouch lay atop a wide stump.

First the warriors danced a war dance, kicking their knees high to the steady "*hi-ya hi-ya*" cadence.

Arrow Keeper prayed to Maiyun while Touch the Sky gave his prayer wings, scattering rich tobacco as an offering to the four directions of the wind. Then the warriors lined up for the solemn ritual of presenting an offering to the Medicine Arrows.

They left skins, weapons, favorite scalps, bright beads, shards of mirror, doeskin wallets and parfleches, quilled moccasins, beaded leggings, brightly dyed feathers, tobacco, long clay pipes. Black Elk carefully avoided Touch the Sky's eyes as he knelt to leave a handsome calico shirt before the stump—this near to the Arrows was no place for hostile thoughts.

Wolf Who Hunts Smiling, however, showed no such restraint. As he rose, after leaving a tow quiver, he whispered for Touch the Sky's ears alone:

"A powerful shaman indeed! Where was his strong medicine to free his faithful friend Little Horse? He is dead by now, medicine man, and all your prayers and incantations are useless!"

These words burned in Touch the Sky's mind like glowing embers, refusing to go out. They still plagued him as the war party, in two long columns singing their battle songs, finally rode out.

The war party rode hard, constantly keeping flankers and point riders out. They all reported the same thing: There was evidence of many shod horses, but no sign of militiamen. Touch the Sky feared this could mean only one thing, that the mercenaries had been summoned to the *Sioux Princess* in expectation of a hard battle.

For two sleeps they rode hard. Touch the Sky had chosen his spirited dun mare, a present from Arrow Keeper. Cheyennes fasted before battle, and now they only gnawed on strips of venison as they rode, swallowing only the juice. They stopped twice to water their horses and sleep for short periods. When they finally crested the last long rise before the Tongue River valley, Touch the Sky's fear became reality.

Far below, still toy-sized in the waning sunlight, was the heavily armed keelboat. And surrounding it was the harrowing sight of a virtual army, dug in for heavy fighting. Scores of militiamen swarmed behind solid breastworks of pointed logs. The boatmen had been ordered to remain in their usual camp on the far bank, armed with carbines as a rearguard force. At this distance Touch the Sky could make out no signs of Little Horse or Old Knobby.

"Brothers, hear me well!" said Black Elk as they camped that night below the crest.

It was a cold camp by strict order, and sentries had been sent out. As was the custom, the attack would commence at dawn and they would attack out of the sun.

"The hair-faces have put up a mighty show of defense. But tomorrow the green grass beside that river will flow red with hair-face blood! They are fighting for nothing but money; *we* fight for the red homeland! Apaches are better fighters than these men. Yet did I not rout the Apache leader Sky Walker and thirty followers from breastworks?"

Several warriors had been at that battle, when Black Elk had only 18 winters behind him. Now one of them said, "You did, Black Elk, I was there!"

Wolf Who Hunts Smiling rose beside his cousin and addressed himself to the junior warriors whom he had recently trained.

"Little brothers, some of you too have seen your fathers and mothers slain by white devils as I have!

Tomorrow you give your enemies a war face. If you must die, and some *will* die, know it will be the glorious death! And when you fall, fall on the bones of a white dog! These are the murderers who exterminate the red man! Little brothers, at first light show the blooded warriors among us that you are eager! I want to see my warriors racing to count first coup!"

Wolf Who Hunts Smiling's eyes had held Touch the Sky's as he said this, issuing a challenge. Touch the Sky held his face impassive, but gave a slight nod—the challenge had been accepted.

Though few would sleep soundly that night, the warriors drank much water as was the custom. Thus, aching bladders would waken them early for the attack. Well before dawn, Touch the Sky was running his weapons and equipment through one final check. Then, as the newborn sun streaked pink the horizon, he rode his dun to the long, curved battle line forming just below the crest.

His last act, as he waited, was to don his magic mountain-lion skin.

The junior warriors were nervous, eager to prove themselves, and more experienced braves held them in check with stern glances and remarks. *Wait for the signal* was the command passed up and down the line.

Black Elk took in a mighty breath, ready to scream the war cry that would signal the attack.

Wolf Who Hunts Smiling met Touch the Sky's glance, his quick eyes mocking the tall brave. Then, before Black Elk could signal, Wolf Who Hunts Smiling dug his knees into the flanks of his pure black pony. His mount leaped forward, already a half-dozen paces downhill when Black Elk's shrill *"Hi-ya hi-i-i-ya!"* sounded.

The curved line surged forward, the war cry filling the air. Their enemy had been prepared for attack for two days. Now the best sharpshooters knelt out front of the others, waiting for the Cheyennes to ride into maximum effective range.

The attackers knew that their best defense across open territory was the agility of the ponies. Riding in a straight line provided an easy target, as did predictable patterns. Now the lead warriors zigzagged in crazy patterns as they rode close enough to send in the first bullets and arrows.

The sharpshooters were amazed—the Cheyennes were so skilled as riders they seemed an extension of their ponies. They bounced with perilous ease, seeming always on the verge of flying off the horse, as they strung their bows or reloaded their rifles. Several sharpshooters fell in that first volley, yet only one Cheyenne pony was hit. The rider leaped up behind another warrior and they escaped.

The success of the first wave heartened the second. While the scattered marksmen were hurrying back further behind their breastworks, the fighting Cheyennes rode close and fired a second fatal volley.

So far, though, no attacker had penetrated the breastworks to count the first coup of the battle. Despite his lead in the attack, Wolf Who Hunts Smiling had been kept busy outriding bullets. Now, as the second wave of Cheyennes fired into the whites, he and Touch the Sky both urged their ponies closer to their enemies.

An opening appeared between the points of two breastworks and Touch the Sky spotted the deck of the keelboat. And his heart leaped into his throat with sudden hope: He couldn't tell if they were dead or alive, but two figures lay staked out on the deck near the plank cabin.

Then his attention returned to the breastworks closer at hand. At the same moment he and Wolf Who Hunts Smiling watched Sam Meeks, the Bluecoat deserter whose testimony had sealed their fate, leap from a rifle pit. He fired at a junior Cheyenne warrior, knocking him from his pony with a fatal hit to the chest.

Touch the Sky dug heels into his pony and leaped over the pointed breastworks from the left; Wolf Who Hunts Smiling kicked his pony into motion and sailed in from the right. The dun was quicker, and Touch the Sky brought his lance down hard on Meeks just a moment before Wolf Who Hunts Smiling tapped him with his rifle.

It was Wolf Who Hunts Smiling who got the kill on his second pass, firing point-blank to avenge their fallen comrade. But as Touch the Sky raced on, toward the *Sioux Princess*, he exulted in the knowledge that Black Elk and others had seen him count first coup.

Behind him, as he deserted his pony now and moved forward from tree to tree on foot, the Cheyenne warriors covered their tribe with glory. Wave after wave assaulted the breastworks now, emboldened by the success of the first attacks. Several more warriors lay dead or dying, but even more white militiamen had been sent under, and more were dying in the unexpectedly fierce attack.

A group had been held in reserve to fight from the keelboat. Touch the Sky couldn't spot Munro, but there was Hays Jackson and Fargo Danford and Heck Nash. All crouched behind barrels and crates, their weapons at the ready.

In the corner of his eye, Touch the Sky saw Wolf Who Hunts Smiling sneak up to a tree beside him. Heck Nash, his attention distracted by the main battle at the breastworks, did not notice the Cheyennes closer at hand. He moved from behind cover to see better.

Wolf Who Hunts Smiling unlashed the throwing tomahawk secured to his legging sash. He had been waiting for this opportunity to avenge himself on the white dog who had made water in his face. He stepped from behind his tree and threw his tomahawk hard. It caught Nash high in the chest and brought him down hard, still alive but blood spurting high from his wound.

"Behind the trees!" shouted Fargo Danford, snapping off a round at Wolf Who Hunts Smiling. But a moment later Danford's hands flew to the hole Black Elk, just now charging the keelboat with several warriors at his heels, shot through his forehead.

Under cover of Black Elk's charge, Touch the Sky and Wolf Who Hunts Smiling also charged the boat. Touch the Sky sent a bullet from his Sharps into the face of a militiaman, then tossed his rifle aside and strung his bow, dropping a second mercenary. He and Wolf Who Hunts Smiling reached the boat at the same time. As Touch the Sky leaped aboard, Wolf paused to scalp Heck Nash while the wounded man, still alive, screamed hideously.

More Cheyenne attackers leaped aboard, and screams filled the air as the bloody fight was reduced to knives and tomahawks. Slashing furiously, his face and hands covered with enemy blood, Touch the Sky fought his way toward the two prisoners staked out on the deck on the far side of the cabin.

He reached them and felt a tight bubble of joy rise into his throat—they were both alive. Battered and bruised and filthy, but alive.

"The hell took you, sprout?" demanded Knobby in a show of bravado. "This deck plays hell on my rheumatic!"

Touch the Sky knelt and sliced through their bonds. But neither one moved at first, muscles locked into position.

"Where's Munro?" Touch the Sky asked Little Horse.

"Hiding in the cabin with his pistols and his talking papers!"

With a mighty victory cry, the Cheyennes at the main battle had routed the last of the militiamen. These were fording the river in retreat. But now a surprise lay in store for them: At a command from Etienne, who until now had kept his men out of the battle, the rearguard of Creole voyageurs was cutting the mercenaries down.

Knobby and Little Horse were finally sitting up, making their first efforts to stand and find better cover. Touch the Sky, intent on reaching the cabin, didn't notice when Hays Jackson suddenly swung one of the swivel-mounted blunderbusses full around and aimed it at him point-blank.

"Brother!" screamed Little Horse, but he was too late. With a deafening roar the blunderbuss fired its eight-ounce ball.

Only Little Horse and Jackson saw a hole appear in the plank wall of the cabin behind Touch the Sky. But instead of falling to the deck, a hole punched through him, Touch the Sky only stared in bewilderment at his unharmed mountain-lion skin—the same skin which Arrow Keeper assured him had strong medicine.

Jackson's jaw fell open in astonishment, and for a fatal moment he was surprised into immobility. The ball couldn't have passed through the Indian; his aim had to have been off.

Little Horse, limping badly on the leg Jackson had ruined with the belaying pin, hobbled to another blunderbuss. Knobby joined him and put a sulphur match to the touch hole. The gun spat fire, and there was a sound like a water bag bursting as the ball tore out Jackson's ample stomach. For a moment he stood rooted, the river behind him visible through the hole in his body, before his ruined carcass collapsed.

Wolf Who Hunts Smiling had already approached the cabin and been sent sprawling by a near-fatal blast from one of the dueling pistols. Now, with the last of the militiamen dead or routed, Touch the Sky called out, "Hold! The white dog cannot go anywhere."

The horses and mules had already been moved to a safe spot downriver. Using hand signals, Touch the Sky cleared everyone off the boat, helping Little Horse ashore. The last thing he did was smash a coal-oil lamp and trail the flammable oil in a line from the boarding ramp to the powder cache just aft of the cabin.

Knobby struck a match with his fingernail and flipped it in the oil. A fast, snaking trail of flame covered the deck, reached the cache, fizzled for a moment. A heartbeat later a deafening explosion obliterated the deck and the cabin, sending planks and ropes and tattered pieces of canvas sail—and fluttering sheets of "private treaties"—sailing off high into the sky.

*   *   *

The Cheyennes held an impromptu scalp dance that night beside the river, thanking Maiyun for this important victory. Only four Cheyenne braves had died, while five times that number of enemies had been slain. Tomorrow they would spend the day helping the Creoles, now their unlikely battle allies, build a crude flatboat so they could return to New Orleans. For their part in helping the Cheyennes, they were given a share of the captured horse herds in addition to their weapons.

Touch the Sky was elated with the victory. But while he was still rejoicing, watching the last smoldering embers of the *Sioux Princess* sink into the river, he was momentarily sobered. As this battle proved, their homeland had been permanently invaded. And as his vision at Medicine Lake had so painfully made real, for the red man, the fighting had just begun. Word of this Tongue River battle would eventually reach the Great White Council and their blue-bloused soldiers. Each victory spawned more bloody battles.

Nor were his personal battles within the tribe over. It wasn't enough for Black Elk that he swore to respect his marriage vows. The war chief also insisted that Touch the Sky somehow give up his love for Honey Eater. That would never happen. Nor would Wolf Who Hunts Smiling be content until one of them crossed over. So let the battles come, he was ready.

Arrow Keeper had spoken the straight word: Touch the Sky would face many trials and much suffering before he raised high the lance of leadership. But Arrow Keeper had also said he was the son of a great Cheyenne chief. That it was his destiny to find greatness just as his father had.

A shadow limped across from the dancers circling the huge victory fire. Touch the Sky turned to his friend.

"Come dance for me, brother," Little Horse said. His leg had been splinted, and he used a hickory-limb crutch. "I would dance with the tribe, but I cannot. I need your legs."

Touch the Sky knew what his friend was doing. He was telling him that it was the white man's way to brood after a great victory. A Cheyenne celebrated with his people.

"Then let us dance, brother!" Touch the Sky said. A moment later a tall Cheyenne warrior took his place among the dancers kicking high about the fire. The others made room as was his due. Something about his manner suggested that none had better challenge him. And none did.

For they had seen him count first coup in the day's great battle, and though he was clearly marked for trouble, all agreed that Touch the Sky was no warrior to trifle with.

Young guns, old-time action!

CHET CUNNINGHAM

The Willy Boy Gang was made up of the youngest lawbreakers on the frontier, but each was ten times as deadly as any man twice his age. All six had a vendetta to settle, and they vowed to ride until every one of them had tasted revenge.

#4: AVENGERS. Headed for Denver, where the Professor had more than one score to even, the Willy Boy Gang planned to drain every cent from the Denver First Colorado Bank and murder any one who stood in their way.

__2896-4 $2.95

#5: RIO GRANDE REVENGE. Deadly *federales* had taken Juan Romero's wife and son hostage. But Romero and the gang would free them — even if they had to drown the corrupt officers in pools of their own blood.

__2967-7 $2.95

#6: FLAGSTAFF SHOWDOWN. In Arizona to save Gunner Johnson's mother from an embezzler, the gang had more than their share of trouble. For the swindler was desperate enough to kill them all — and crazy enough to succeed.

__3154-X $2.95 US/$3.95 CAN

LEISURE BOOKS
ATTN: Order Department
276 5th Avenue, New York, NY 10001

Please add $1.50 for shipping and handling for the first book and $.35 for each book thereafter. N.Y.S. and N.Y.C. residents, please add appropriate sales tax. No cash, stamps, or C.O.D.s. All orders shipped within 6 weeks via postal service book rate. Canadian orders require $2.00 extra postage. It must also be paid in U.S. dollars through a U.S. banking facility.

Name _____

Address _____

City _____ State _____ Zip _____

I have enclosed $_____ in payment for the checked book(s).
Payment <u>must</u> accompany all orders. ☐ Please send a free catalog.

DOUBLE WESTERNS
A Double Blast of
Rip-roarin' Western Action!

TWO CLASSIC TALES OF ACTION
AND ADVENTURE
IN THE OLD WEST
FOR THE PRICE OF ONE.
One Heck of a Value!

TRAIL TO HIGH PINE/WEST OF THE BARBWIRE
By Lee Floren.
_3183-3 $4.50

CHEYENNE GAUNTLET/INDIAN TERRITORY
By David Everitt.
_3194-9 $4.50

GUNSHOT TRAIL/TEXAS TORNADO
By Nelson Nye.
_3234-1 $4.50

BROOMTAIL BASIN/TRAIL TO GUNSMOKE
By Lee Floren.
_3262-7 $4.50

LEISURE BOOKS
ATTN: Order Department
276 5th Avenue, New York, NY 10001

Please add $1.50 for shipping and handling for the first book and $.35 for each book thereafter. N.Y.S. and N.Y.C. residents, please add appropriate sales tax. No cash, stamps, or C.O.D.s. All orders shipped within 6 weeks via postal service book rate. Canadian orders require $2.00 extra postage. It must also be paid in U.S. dollars through a U.S. banking facility.

Name _____

Address _____

City _____ State _____ Zip _____

I have enclosed $_____in payment for the checked book(s).
Payment <u>must</u> accompany all orders.□ Please send a free catalog.

CHEYENNE

JUDD COLE

Follow the adventures of Touch the Sky as he searches for a world he can call his own!

#1: Arrow Keeper. Born Indian, raised white, Touch the Sky longs to find his place among his own people. But he will need a warrior's courage, strength, and skill to battle the enemies who would rather see him die than call him brother.

_3312-7 $3.50 US/$4.50 CAN

#2: Death Chant. Feared and despised by his tribe, Touch the Sky must prove his loyalty to the Cheyenne before they will accept him. And when the death chant arises, he knows if he fails he will not die alone.

_3337-2 $3.50 US/$4.50 CAN

Two Classic Westerns
In One Rip-roaring Volume!
A $7.00 Value For Only 4.50!

"These Westerns are written by the hand of a master!"
—New York *Times*

LAST TRAIN FROM GUN HILL/THE BORDER GUIDON
__3361-5 $4.50

BARRANCA/JACK OF SPADES
__3384-4 $4.50

BRASADA/BLOOD JUSTICE
__3410-7 $4.50